The Passenger Manifest

Rebecca Southgate Williams

Copyright © 2024 Rebecca Southgate Williams

The moral right of Rebecca Southgate Williams to be recognised as the creator of this original work is hereby certified. All rights reserved. No part of this publication may be reproduced, distributed, or transmitted in any form or by any means, including photocopying, recording, or other electronic or mechanical methods, without the prior written permission of the author or the publisher, except in the case of brief quotations embodied in critical reviews, and certain other non-commercial uses where permitted by local legislation.

NO AI TRAINING: Without in any way limiting the author's exclusive rights under copyright, any use of this publication to "train" generative artificial intelligence (AI) technologies to generate text is expressly prohibited. The author reserves all rights to license uses of this work for generative AI training and development of machine learning language models.

This is a work of fiction, all characters, places, and entities are fictional or are used in a fictional setting. Any resemblance for the fictional characters to persons living or deceased is entirely coincidental.

Design and layout by Oliver Tooley
Cover design by Paul Dixon

ISBN: 9798340526243

For my daughter, Isabelle, who will read this.
And for my sons, Ben and Tom, who probably won't.

For life goes not backward nor tarries with yesterday.
You are the bows from which your children as living arrows are sent forth.
The archer sees the mark upon the path of the infinite, and He bends you
with His might that His arrows may go swift and far.

Kahlil Gibran, The Prophet, 1923

Chapter One
Daughter

...and I have to think out tricks to fool them with.
The first was a real inspiration. I set up a great web on
my loom here and started weaving....

— *Homer, The Odyssey, Book 19*

She bit her lip and strode forward.
Keep on moving. Keep on keeping on.
Her honed mantra.

The platform was sparsely populated, a smattering of passengers peppered along its anodyne length. She forged her way purposefully ahead, eyes surreptitiously scanning for co-travellers she might know - keen to avoid eye contact, keen to dodge connection. As she passed the overhead information board, she checked her early morning train was on time. Establishing that, against all odds, it was, she checked the zones to ensure she was heading in the right direction for First Class. She was ever mindful of how irritatingly frequently the train seemed to arrive with a configuration reversed from its advertised form, leaving her scurrying from one end of the platform to the other. Boarding and making her way through the train just wasn't an option for her. Senses on high alert, she readied herself for this familiar journey.

She had been making this journey for the past fifteen years, having relocated from a swanky London borough to a sleepy Devon hamlet. Bringing up children in London, no matter how privileged their circumstances, was no match for the freedom they had to roam Devon's shores and moors. Visiting her mother, who still lived in one of the capital's leafy suburbs, had, until more recently, been a welcome diversion from the daily demands of her family life. Now that the boys had simultaneously flown the proverbial nest, she should have felt freer, less bound, and yet she felt more tethered than ever. Whereas once it was the time spent with her mother which had revitalised and reinvigorated her, it was now the journey alone which provided some temporary respite. Caught between the tattered binds of one life and the creeping bonds of another, this voyage afforded her a cocoon of refuge. However fraught, tense, preoccupied she might feel on entering the station, she knew that as soon as she had found her seat, she could begin to unravel and enter her own space.

To her relief, the train was quiet, and she had a table to herself; the seat opposite was unreserved, and with luck would remain vacant for a good part of the journey up to London. The adjacent table was unoccupied, with three reservations from Taunton. She hoped she would have a good hour with no distraction and no interruption, save the welcome provision of refreshments. The evening before had been unnerving and heavily charged; she badly needed a little time to just be, to exhale. The half hour drive to the station at Totnes had afforded her time to stew over words spoken and glances exchanged at the dinner party the night before. She determined to rid her mind of all these unwelcome distractions for now, enter her safe space, and inhabit the present.

As the train pulled out of the station, she switched her phone to silent, pausing only to glance at her sons on the screensaver, before dropping it into her bag. She closed

Chapter One - Daughter

her eyes, emptied her mind and 'let the train take the strain'.

Just as she was beginning to feel her shoulders drop and a welcome somnolence creep over her, a voice at her shoulder broke in, "Any refreshments for you today, Madam?"

A welcome distraction.

"Oooh, yes please. Tea, please. White, no sugar."

"Certainly, Madam. Anything else with that?"

Her standard answer, "No, thank you. Not today."

Never deviating from her strict regime ensured she maintained the weight of her youth. Her discipline was iron, her body taut.

The train pushing on through Newton Abbot and then up through the Teign estuary to the Exe, she sipped her tea, feasting her eyes on the beauty of the ever-shifting landscape with its green rolling hills, intertidal mudflats, winding creeks, red sandstone cliffs, and vast expanses of estuary and sea. As she gazed intently through the streaky glass of the train window, the early morning mists started to dissipate, revealing the sultry tones of the season - the conker browns, gamboge yellows and flaming reds of autumn which never ceased to delight her. Their vibrancy stark against crisp, blue skies, or piercing through the greyest of days - no matter the weather, this would always be her favourite time of year.

Stopping at Exeter St David's always felt like a gateway into a different terrain - leaving behind the plodding pace of her parochial life and crossing into a new land promising vigour and vitality the further the train progressed. At times, she relished this. At times, she lacked the energy to engage.

This morning, drained from lack of sleep and the tormented ruminations of the night, she braced herself for the journey beyond the gateway. Girding herself to behold the crush and rush of early morning commuters on the platform, she reminded herself of her First Class privilege. Rarely, even on this commuter train to London Paddington, was the carriage so full as to be uncomfortable. She doubted her cocoon would be so congenial were she to share it with the hoi polloi. Fleetingly, she wondered when she had become so entitled.

As besuited and conservatively chic commuters settled into seats, she observed with detachment the fussing and fiddling around her as damp coats were peeled off, misty glasses cleaned, hair smoothed down or puffed up, laptops uncased, chargers plugged in, headsets donned, earbuds inserted, smartphones checked. At this time of day her travel companions were predictably executive in style and manner. She recognised that she sat apart; her understated expensive capsule wardrobe segregating her from the makeshift office environment around her. Her cream cashmere sweater, designer jeans, calf leather footwear and Bottega Veneta bag afforded her an air of opulence and indulgence. She became suddenly and keenly aware of the gaping gulf between her and them; her recent life transition into relative indolence juxtaposing with the hive of activity around her.

Until the departure of her twin boys a year ago, her life had been a familiar term-time whirl of school runs, club pickups, PTA duties, punishing gym sessions, yoga classes, oat milk lattes, lunch dates and dinner parties. The only punctuation to this relentless routine was the monthly trip to see her mother. Term-time was

Chapter One - Daughter

predictable, manageable, formulaic. Holiday time, in its own way, was more of the same in different locations. Whether UK breaks or far-flung exotic holidays, the schedule had always been designed around the prevailing needs and desires of her husband and sons.

As the train snaked its way through green fields from Exeter to Taunton, she began to reflect upon her current situation. Over the past couple of years, the plates of her life had been slowly shifting. She wondered, not for the first time, where they might settle.

On the approach into Taunton Station, her reverie was cut short by the dulcet tones of the train manager's voice. Earlier announcements had been of the automated kind. She smiled to herself; she recognised this voice.

A very welcome distraction.

This particular train manager's voice was almost theatrical and his wit sharp; he brightened the traveller's day and his own, no doubt, with just the right tone and humour.

"Ladies and Gentlemen, our next stop is the bustling market town of Taunton. The weather today is rather inclement, so don't forget your brolly and galoshes. Please ensure you take all your luggage and personal belongings with you. And don't forget any dogs or children, whether you intend to or not!"

A snigger went around the carriage.

No-one moved. No dogs, no children here. These hard-bitten commuters were ensconced for the long haul, either alighting at Paddington or at Reading maybe for an airport connection. She glanced at the table opposite.

Would the reserved seats now be occupied? Or maybe no-shows?

Her question was soon answered as a well-dressed older couple, having unburdened themselves of their suitcases, made their way along the carriage, peering myopically at seat numbers.

"Here they are, Lydia," a balding sixty something said as he approached. "Would you like to sit by the window?"

"Thanks love, yes. Oh good, forward-facing," Lydia answered.

Lydia obviously had the same issue as her - travelling backwards induced nausea. She always ensured she booked forward facing seats. She afforded them a muted smile and nod as they settled in their seats. Like her, they clearly were not commuters; they unpacked novels, crossword books, pens, and The Telegraph.

She loved to ponder on the likely stories of her fellow travellers; who they might be; where they might be heading. This couple were well-heeled, well-presented, and yet somehow well-worn. She imagined they had been married since their youth; he had worked in finance; she had been a homemaker. Now, in early retirement, they spent their days on committees, at Pilates, on the golf course, looking after grandchildren, and taking city breaks, winter sun holidays and extended cruises.

Echoes of life to come?

Her heart sank just a little.

Just as the couple had marked their territory with books, pens, newspaper and the ubiquitous smartphones, a younger woman, early thirties she guessed, entered the carriage. She seemed to enter all at once, a ball of energy and life, arriving at their table with a flourish, plonking a large crimson bucket bag on one

Chapter One - Daughter

seat and hoisting her jaunty yellow cabin luggage onto the overhead rack.

Definitely going to the airport.

Her interest piqued just a little.

As the young woman settled herself, the refreshment trolley came by once again. She pre-empted the question, "A coffee, please. Black, no milk, no sugar."

"Anything else, Madam?"

She replied, as usual, in the negative. She wouldn't eat until lunchtime, never breaking her well-practised habit. Never veering off course. Her stomach rumbled ever so slightly.

As the steward turned to the table opposite, both the young woman and older couple signalled their desire for refreshment too.

"Oh, you first," urged the younger woman. A soft Irish lilt. "I'm still deciding."

"Thank you," said Lydia's husband. And turning to the steward, "Two coffees, milk for both, sugar for one. And two slices of the fruit cake please."

"Righto sir, coming up." He served the older couple and then waited for further instruction from the younger woman, his gaze lingering just a little too long on ample cleavage.

"Oh, me now. Yep, great. Coffee with milk and sugar, and the shortbread, please. And I'll have some salt and vinegar crisps, and a bottle of water." Looking at the older couple, "Might as well go for the full experience seeing as it's complimentary! As if that makes up for the ticket price!" she snorted. Flashing the steward a winning smile, she turned once more to the couple and introduced herself.

"Hello, I'm Aisling. I'll be with you until Reading."

I knew it.

Aisling was undoubtedly heading off on an adventure. Discreetly, she repositioned herself ever so slightly in order to tune into the conversation which would surely ensue. Other people's lives held a growing fascination for her the older she got and the less encumbered her own life became.

Her repositioning afforded her a better view of the young woman opposite - attractive in a pulpy, doughy way: soft squidgy skin, voluptuous curves, and a porcelain complexion. A shock of tousled black ringlets lent her an air of romance and enchantment. And she was obviously confident, self-assured; announcing her presence and introducing herself in such a presumptive way. She was intrigued to hear more from Aisling.

"We're on until London," said Lydia. "Visiting our daughter and her family," politely offering just a little more information. Her husband's head was bowed, his reading glasses on, crossword and pen at the ready.

"Oh, grand. That'll be nice. I love catching up with family, me. Happens far too rarely for my liking. C'est la vie, I suppose."

"Where are you off to?" Lydia enquired, her husband settling into his crossword puzzle, leaving her to engage with the stranger opposite.

"Hamburg."

Well, I didn't expect that, she thought shifting round just a little more.

She looks far more suited to Rome or Barcelona for a city break. Berlin maybe, but Hamburg?

Lydia's husband, head raised, antennae bristling, spoke before his wife could answer.

Chapter One - Daughter

"How interesting, we lived there many moons ago. What takes you to Hamburg?"

"Work," a brief reply. Turning her attention fully to Lydia she enquired, " Where does your daughter live?"

"Oh, she lives in Walthamstow. Quite a shift for her after having grown up in Somerset but she loves it. She stayed on after university and has made London her home. Juggling working in the city with young children. Wouldn't be my cup of tea but she's happy," Lydia was clearly proud of her daughter - the tone of her voice, however, revealed something deeper; a sense of loss, abandonment even.

"Ah," said Aisling, "Nice. Used to be a bit of a dump back in the day but totally hip now. Friends of my parents have lived there for aeons. Their house price has shot through the roof. Must be loaded to have bought there."

I like this woman.

She warmed to her ebullient manner and way of instantly articulating exactly what she felt.

She's a breath of fresh air in the carriage.

Lydia simply smiled thinly and murmured her agreement. Her husband took on the mantle, determined to delve a little deeper.

"So, do you know Hamburg? Have you been before?"

"I've been once before."

Cogs whirring, recollection stirring, he pressed on. "Do you travel regularly for work?"

She nodded.

"We love travelling," he said. "We lived abroad for a number of years before settling back in the UK for our children's schooling. And we travel when we can now, don't we Lyd?" he added, turning to his wife.

I knew it. city breaks, winter sun holidays and extended cruises.

"Budapest next," Lydia confirmed. "Always a travel plan on the horizon with Henry here."

"Oh, Budapest is simply delightful, you'll absolutely love it. A feast for the eyes and senses. Definitely in my top five city break destinations."

She listened as Aisling rattled off a number of must-sees and must-dos for the couple with great enthusiasm. She'd been herself many years ago with her husband, a short break away on their own, leaving her valiant mother single-handedly in charge of their preschool twins. Aisling's exuberant passion struck a chord with her - stirring up something deep within. She, too, had been charmed by Budapest, by its beautiful architecture, rich culture, sumptuous fin-de-siècle coffee houses, and the beautiful Danube dissecting the very heart of the city, separating the Buda Hills on the western bank from the Pest Plains on the eastern bank. She had marvelled at how the two halves contrasted enormously in character and terrain, vying for her attention, courting her favour.

Not unlike my boys.

It occurred to her now that her enjoyment of it had, however, been somewhat contained. Less immersive than Aisling's. Less ardent.

As the ping pong of conversation continued between the newly formed trio opposite, she was drawn further into Aisling's world, Aisling's outlook. She found herself becoming fascinated by this attractive, vibrant, sassy young woman not, she imagined, many years her junior.

A direct question from Henry temporarily halted the ping pong, "Tell me," looking directly at Aisling. "You're not Aisling Rourke are you?"

Chapter One - Daughter

Aisling squinted at him, holding his gaze, pausing for a few beats. Lowering her voice to a conspiratorial hush, she said, "I am indeed."

"Aha, I knew it!" he exclaimed, clearly proud of his powers of observation.

Well done Sherlock, the profile photo alongside my blog was a big enough clue, Aisling did well to hide her disdain.

"I'm a big fan of your Telegraph travel blog. Inspired me to book many an adventure."

"Thank you. Pays the bills and allows me to indulge my passions," she responded graciously.

As the conversation picked up pace once again, travel stories were swapped, humorous anecdotes recounted, and recommendations given. Henry's initial disinterest in the stranger opposite had morphed into a probing, somewhat brazen, curiosity. Lydia had been relegated to the fringes of the conversation, from where she only managed to interject the odd question or observation.

Drawn deeper and deeper into the animated dialogue opposite, she could not help but compare herself with Aisling. She, too, was well-travelled and well-versed in culture and history. And yet an unassailable chasm seemed to separate them. She was enchanted by Aisling's vigour and energy, her appetite for life. She was disenchanted by her own creeping lethargy.

What has happened to me? Where's my oomph? My sense of self?

Whilst Aisling was living out her dreams, she, by contrast, now seemed to walk through life in a dull slumber. She felt as if she was staring into an abyss; an encroaching nightmare of fruitlessness and futility.

All at once, the irony of her name struck her. Her mother had so carefully chosen it: a maternal vision, a desire for her only child to weave her dreams into the fabric of her earthbound life.

A dream weaver. A bright vision. High hopes.

And yet, now, just over a year shy of her fortieth birthday, it occurred to her that aspirations and ambitions, once so tightly woven, were nothing but broken yarns and loose ends.

As the train ploughed on towards Reading and the terrain shifted once more, granting charming views of the Kennet and Avon Canal, her focus swerved from Aisling's story to her own.

Well-travelled, well-heeled, well-groomed, and well-nigh stultified, her life's story had been woven around a whirlwind romance and unplanned pregnancy. Intoxicated by the attentions of an attractive older man and swept along on an exhilarating wave of romance, she had turned her back on her once imagined future. Her sterling A Level results had secured her a place to study Classics at Durham University but, to her mother's great chagrin, she never went. She had met her husband on her gap year travelling around the Greek islands and the rest was, of course, history. She was, she now knew, just his type; long Titian hair, piercing green eyes, a smattering of freckles across her nose, and a long, lean dancer's body. He was seduced by her looks; she by his charisma, attention, and wealth. Having been raised by a single mother, finances had been tight and their lifestyle frugal. Life with him held the promise of indulgence; high-end living, exotic holidays, adventure. When, after a few short months together, he asked her to marry him, the decision wasn't difficult. And the Cartier solitaire sealed the deal.

Chapter One - Daughter

Had she not fallen pregnant shortly before her marriage, she wondered if things may have been different. Would her carnal appetites have been sated? Would she have elected once again to study, look outside herself, broaden her perspectives, carve out a career? Weave a different tapestry?

Do I regret my boys?

Flashing through her mind, this unwelcome thought caught her by surprise. Inwardly, she recoiled in horror. Never had she thought she might regret, resent even, her twin sons. Even during the eight and a half long months of protracted hyperemesis, when nausea and vomiting were her constant bedfellows, did it occur to her that she didn't want her babies. Was the pregnancy unplanned? Yes. Were the babies unwanted? Absolutely not. Revisiting it now, it was clear this truth remained and yet, regret was there. Regret not for the birth of her sons, but for another life lost.

Indeed, her boys, young men now of nineteen and going into their second year at university, were still for her a raison d'être.

For how much longer though?

Already, she could see them slowly loosening the threads connecting them to their parents; each disentangling himself in his own way. Incrementally, they spent less holiday time at home or away en famille, and more with friends, new and old. She knew this was inevitable, desirable even, and yet she felt increasingly bereft.

Although identical, the boys could not be more different. She would often marvel at how they could look so alike, even she sometimes struggled to tell them apart in a photograph, but at how dissimilar they were. One egg split to form two such disparate personalities destined to live distinctly different lives. The essence of who they were as unique as their own fingerprints.

Both boys added depth and colour to the achromatic tableau of her home life. Each his own distinct hue.

Will, the more vibrant, more colourful of her sons.

My peacock.

Luke, more muted in tone, with hidden depths.

My dove.

Even as a baby, Will was a force to be contended with. She could have sworn he was the more active in the womb, keeping her up half the night in the final trimester before vigorously pushing his way out of it a full eleven minutes before the coaxed arrival of his brother. Will was a doughty toddler; adventurous and headstrong. As a young man, he is gregarious and flamboyant. Some would say colourful, others, his brother for example, flash.

Luke, by contrast, was a settled, calm baby and a more intuitive, sober child. As a young man, he is the more introspective and more thoughtful of the two. Eclipsed at times by Will, she could discern the charm of Luke's more subtle tones.

Her reflections were broken abruptly by a kerfuffle opposite as Aisling loudly exclaimed, "Shit, I need to get off!"

Having been deep in conversation with Henry and Lydia, and ironically oblivious to instructions for onward travel, Aisling had realised that the train had just pulled into Reading station. Hurried goodbyes and scrabbling for luggage ensued as the travel blogger hastily made her way to the carriage exit, pushing past those who had just boarded, and propelled herself and her luggage through

Chapter One - Daughter

the train door and onto the platform just in the nick of time. A moment later, the doors signalled they were closing.

She watched enviously as Aisling headed off on her next escapade; her life a well-rewarded odyssey. Aisling's retreating figure somehow snagged a hole in the fabric of the carriage. A bare patch.

As the train began the final leg of this particular journey, the train manager resumed his razor-sharp, sing-song repartee, "And a very warm welcome to those of you journeying with us from Reading this morning as we head into the Big Smoke. Whether you're venturing in for business or pleasure, visiting loved ones, escaping unloved ones, or even breaking out the other side to pastures new, do sit back, relax, and enjoy the ride. If you're hoping for a morning coffee or croissant, too late I'm afraid. Them's the breaks. Our onboard buffet service has closed for today, but baristas, bakers and fast food operators await you at Paddington. Our arrival time is 10.29, and with God's speed and a bit of luck, we'll be on time this morning."

This time sniggers were, no doubt. accompanied by harrumphs in second class at the buffet's closure. The First Class cognoscente could simply snigger, knowing they would still receive table service. Conversation dried up, Lydia and Henry sipped their final coffees before disembarkation.

Now, without distraction and rapidly approaching London, the unwelcome thoughts she had successfully held at bay slowly resurfaced. She couldn't help but be pulled back into the scenario played out around her dinner table the evening before. Once again, she felt the gnawing suspicion and tight grip of jealousy. She had been so looking forward to catching up with old friends over supper. Most dinner parties were dull for her; her husband's older friends and connections generally bored her, and it was rare she would invite anyone herself. But she liked Chris and Sarah. He was engaging and funny and she was warm, earthy, almost maternal towards her. What she hadn't bargained for was Matilda, their eldest daughter.

When Sarah had asked if Tilly could join them for the evening, she hadn't hesitated to say yes. She hadn't laid eyes on Tilly for a long time; it would be good to reconnect with her properly. She had occasionally caught glimpses of her cycling or driving through the village on her brief visits when down from university. It must have been a good few years since she had seen her up close and personal. Tilly, or Matilda as she now preferred, the once gawky, slip of a girl was now a sleek, stylish young woman. She'd been living with her parents for a couple of months since simultaneously finishing her PhD and dissolving a long-term relationship in the summer. It had been messy; he was a serial cheater, breaking her heart over and over again. This was a fresh start. Sarah had confided in her that Tilly had been devastated, struggling to find a way forward but, more recently, had begun to find her feet, refocused.

She really has refocused, she thought sardonically.

It wasn't so much the way Matilda now looked that troubled her, it was the way her husband studiously didn't look too long at Matilda and the way he and Matilda stole glances at one another which unsettled her.

She had long become accustomed to her husband's roving eye. Whereas once she naively believed his eye was for her alone, she had become ever more aware that

Chapter One - Daughter

the older she became, the less he looked. His eye was drawn to younger, more nubile women; lingering looks lasting just that little bit longer; moving down from fresh faces to trace the soft curves of their bodies; mentally undressing each one for his pleasure. Every time she noticed this, a little bit inside her died a quiet death. She never dared challenge him, more for fear of what he would reveal than for how he might react.

What she once saw as romantic, the older sophisticated man falling for a girl half his age was now irreparably tainted. Now that she was pushing forty and he a few years shy of sixty, she would see him turn to ogle women not only half his age but also a third of his age.

When did this slippery slope start? When did I first notice? Has it always been like this?

What was once arcane and profound was now prosaic and shallow. The romance and passion of their life together had slowly and invidiously been replaced by an omertà shrouding the jading of their desire for one another.

With a growing realisation of her fading youth and her husband's unfading appetites, she had, of course, harboured an unspoken suspicion that these appetites were being sated elsewhere. She had become accustomed to the business trips and nights away; they had been part of the fabric of their married life from the outset. During the early years, her hands were full enough and the sex good enough for her not to even suspect he might play away. As the years went by, their marriage had hit hurdles, and their sex life had faltered at times. Suspicions were aroused within her, but any snags or tears in their relationship were soon patched up. In more recent years, the snags seemed more pronounced and the tears wider. He no longer seemed to return to her with reinvigorated passion. A knot tightened slowly in her stomach.

Is something happening right under my nose? Something I can't ignore?

She forced these unwelcome thoughts from her mind. She couldn't face contemplating what his growing disinterest might mean, and what it could lead to. She must focus, look forward. She would need all her energy, all her mental strength, for the time with her mother.

She knew this journey like the back of her hand; a peregrination religiously observed for the past decade and a half. In this final stage of the first leg, the train would slip further and further away from the rich countryside palette; fields, woodlands and waterways replaced by industrial units, warehouses, offices, and tenement blocks. A landscape shifting from rural to urban as steel and concrete encroached. Her senses would always resharpen, her breathing quicken as she reluctantly uncoupled herself from the steady, familiar, soothing pulse of the train and braced herself for the push across the city until she was eventually disgorged into the suburb of her youth.

Up until a few years ago, she would stay with her mother in her childhood home. Her bedroom would still embrace her, the detritus of teenage years cleared away but the room still very much hers; another cocoon. Now that the house had been sold for her mother's care costs, she would book into a local hotel overnight. She had marvelled at how the tiny terrace house had sold for such a vast sum of money. What was once the modest domain of a single mother and her only child had skyrocketed in

Chapter One - Daughter

value with the gentrification of this once unremarkable suburban neighbourhood.

As she prepared to cross London this morning, she wondered what she could expect from the time with her mother. It could change from one day to the next on her two day visit. Her mother had been her constant; a stable presence, a grounding anchor. Always there, always available, always rooted.

I would have loved my own daughter, she brooded, not for the first time.

A friend, confidante, ally.

It was not to be. A deep wound festered.

With the Alzheimer diagnosis eight years ago, her mother had been slowly slipping away from her, from their life together. Now anchor up, she was drifting. She recalled how on the last visit, her mother failed to recognise her, hitting her away, hissing at her. Each time her mother didn't perceive her, didn't recall who she was and what they meant to one another, her sense of self shrivelled just that little bit more.

Now on the approach to Paddington, she catches a glimpse of her reflected image in the darkened window; her picture-perfect profile; the carefully styled sweep of her hair; the glint of a pearl earring. The shell of who she is. But not, maybe, the essence of who she would like to be.

She gathers herself for the onward journey and for the two days ahead. For now, she is a daughter.

Chapter Two
Emma

There are only two sorts of doctors: those who practise with their brains, and those who practise with their tongues.

—William Osler

Heart racing, hood up, head down and clutching her overnight bag, Emma pushed through wind and driving rain across the car park, over the bridge and on to Platform 2, with just a minute or two to spare before the scheduled arrival of the 10.42 to London Paddington.

Oh, for goodness' sake, she groaned inwardly.

Peering from under her dripping hood, she saw, from the overhead train information board, that her train was late just as she heard the announcer's voice utter those all too familiar words, "We are sorry to announce the late arrival of ......" A twenty minute wait. A frustration exacerbated by the fraught journey through wind, rain, and traffic-snarled lanes.

Bloody holidaymakers.

Factoring in the squally weather and poor driving conditions, she thought she had allowed herself plenty of time for the half-hour journey to the station. What she had failed to make allowances for, however, were the October half-term holidaymakers. Whilst she loved where she lived, she was not quite so enamoured that others loved it too. Flocking in their droves in spring and summer, they were the bane of her life as she attempted to make her way out of the sleepy hamlet in which she

Chapter Two - Emma

lived to the nearest town, Kingsbridge. She reluctantly accepted that this was the price she had to pay for living in such a sought-after location.

The irony. I am, after all, a blow-in myself.

The recent pandemic had exacerbated the frustration and exasperation of the locals trying to go about their everyday lives. With so many fun-seekers and sunseekers unable or unwilling to jet off abroad, Devon pulled in converts from all over the UK as they discovered or rediscovered its beauty and attractions. Heavy holiday traffic, no longer confined to spring and summer, clogged up the highways and byways causing chaos and gridlock. Locals despaired as city slickers in Chelsea tractors failed to navigate the country's maze of lanes, bottlenecking long lines of beachbound traffic and mobbing moors.

She cursed herself for forgetting that the vast influx of grockels was no longer largely confined to the lighter, warmer months but had now migrated into the autumn and winter holidays too.

As she waited, she noted that the train too would be congested, with families heading most likely to Exeter for the day. Museums, underground passages, and fast food restaurants were all good options for parents keen to keep their offspring entertained and out of trouble on a blustery October day. All had been her saviour when on Alice duty in rainy school holidays.

Gratitude started to edge out frustration as Emma reminded herself that she would be travelling First Class to the conference. There were some perks to working away from her family during the school holidays. As much as she would have loved to spend time on Alice duty, she knew that Patrick would have an action-packed, fun-filled plan for their time together. Alice would be in her element with him. A little envy crept in. She quickly dismissed it, focusing on the freedom she now had; a temporary reprieve from the ever increasing workload of patient care, partnership stresses and domestic duties. She resolved to make the most of her time at the conference and the journey there and back. It wasn't often she had First Class privileges. She would never have spent her own hard-earned cash on a mediocre upgrade. At least the inflated prices ensured she wouldn't be crammed in with the half-term family day trippers and packs of teenagers set loose for the day.

Boarding the delayed train and making her way to her seat, Emma began to relax. Peeling off her dripping coat, she turned her attention to her hair, capturing and taming the flyaways which had escaped from her sleek ponytail. Taking out her vanity mirror, she studied her face for signs of smudged mascara and hairline frizz. Face blotted, minor infractions sorted, nude lipstick carefully applied, she looked with some pleasure at the end result. She assessed this woman looking back at her. Polished, professional, poised. A woman on a mission. Dressed for the part.

As she took out her iPhone to check for messages, BBC Breaking News flashed across her screen. A brief glance - mention of the King. A slight jolt.

It's still quite weird. The King.

No staunch royalist, Emma had been surprised how the death of the Queen had affected her. She had actually felt a little out of kilter, uncharacteristically emotional. The death of any other ninety-six-year-old woman wouldn't have unsettled her in the least. In her line of work, she was more surprised when someone reached that age. And yet, this particular woman had been part of

Chapter Two - Emma

the backdrop of her life. Part of her tapestry. Almost imperceptibly interwoven. In her own relatively short time on the planet, Emma had only known Elizabeth as Monarch. A Queen without a King. Simply a Prince, a Duke. Never a King.

The plates were moving. The sands shifting. Uncharted territories.

As a woman of science and reason, death was simply the completion of life for Emma.

No more, no less.

An ending.

A full stop.

Yet she recognised how a death also heralded a new beginning for some; a new order; a new chapter; new opportunities even.

Privy to the reactions and emotions of so many facing their own demise, be it imminent or slow in coming, Emma had witnessed a whole spectrum of responses: shock, fear, panic, resignation, acceptance, disbelief, relief. Some patients travelled their final journey with quiet dignity, some railed loudly and angrily against it. Some were loved and supported. Others were alone and afraid. Some were alone, albeit surrounded. Others were held, albeit alone. The much-publicised faith of the Queen would, Emma guessed, have granted her a measure of peace. She had witnessed this with some of her patients. A peace passing all understanding.

This morning, revisiting her recent emotions, she wondered about the hole she herself might leave; with Patrick, Alice, her parents, friends, patients. What would that look like? An Emma-shaped hole. She suspected, hoped rather selfishly, it would be gaping.

She had always felt secure of her place, a round peg in a round hole; a lynchpin in her family, community, and workplace. She was confident, self-assured; self-satisfied some might say. Her passing would undoubtedly leave a vacuum.

Morbid introspection interrupted, "Refreshments for you today, Madam?"

She ordered her drink and thanked the steward, turning her attention away from her future death to her life right now. Swiping Breaking News from her screen, she checked her messages.

Having replied to those messages she couldn't strategically ignore, Emma unzipped her laptop case, plugged in the laptop, and googled the conference. It had been a good few years now since she had attended a medical conference in person. It was a relief not to have to Zoom in. She was sure her eyesight had deteriorated with the surfeit of screen-based work over the past couple of years.

She browsed the programme for the following day as the train pushed on through wind and heavy rain; the dramatic backdrop of slate grey skies and steely, wave-cresting seas drawing her eyes every now and then from the screen before her. She savoured the last moments of her time alone, aware that the seat opposite her would be occupied from Exeter to Paddington.

As the train pulled into St David's, she rechecked her reflection in the mirror, smoothed her brows, touched up her lipstick and prepared to put her best face forward with her fellow traveller.

Hopefully not a bore.

An exodus of second-class passengers tumbled from the carriages, joined by a handful from First Class. The

Chapter Two - Emma

platform was awash with already frazzled families, disparate groups of boisterous, awkward, excitable, or too cool for school teenagers, plus the odd lone traveller. Moving en masse for the stairs to the exit, she watched as they dispersed leaving their successors space to board.

Her quiet carriage sprang to life as groups of people negotiated their way through the aisle, seeking out their seats.

I'm glad I reapplied that lipstick.

The man with his eye on the reservation opposite her was pretty easy on her eye. Mid-forties she guessed, a silver fox. Taking off his raincoat, the silver fox slid into the seat opposite, greeting her with a self-assured smile. She noticed he didn't wear a ring.

She smiled back and looked away out of the window, proffering her profile view. She had him until London. Striking up a conversation could wait awhile.

The fact that she and Patrick had never felt the need to marry, put her at a distinct advantage in certain situations. Unencumbered by the bands of betrothal, she was free to present herself however the fancy may take her.

Not that I'd ever really betray Patrick. A little flirtation maybe.... a little fantasy....

The silver fox took out his smartphone and plugged the charger in. She stole a glance as it sprang to life, revealing a screensaver of two young boys, grinning from ear to ear. Both had his deep-set hazel eyes.

Divorcee, maybe? Or just not married? Or just no ring?

Somehow, it seemed to her that he was most definitely a divorcee. He was too well-groomed, too bright-eyed, too composed to be living with young children. Very well-groomed, in fact.

A divorcee on the pull?

The refreshment trolley pulled up alongside them and he deferred to her.

"You first." A warm-toned, agreeable voice.

Keen to engage with me.

"Oh, I'm good, thanks," she responded. "I've not long had a drink."

"In that case," he proclaimed, turning to the steward, "I'll take a coffee, black, no sugar and a flapjack too."

Turning back to Emma, "Not tempted?"

I am, she thought wryly.

"No, I'm good," she replied, smiling.

Thanking the steward, he turned once again to Emma. "Going all the way?"

She smiled, unsure of whether he was being deliberately suggestive.

Better err on the side of caution.

"I'm on until Paddington. I see you are too."

"Heading back to the office in London, I've been in Exeter overnight for work, for my sins. Glad to get back up there to be honest. Bit backwater down here for me. No offence if you're from Exeter."

"None taken," her response. "What do you do?"

"Family law barrister. Wig and gown and all that pomp. Much happier when dressing up!"

She clocked a slightly arrogant curl of the lip as he spoke.

Clearly rather self-important.

She listened, with very little interest, as he proceeded to talk about himself for the next few minutes, barely pausing for breath.

Chapter Two - Emma

Actually, a bore.

Emma had come across this type of man so many times before: at medical school, at conferences, at the surgery. Puffed up, preening, prosaic. And, so often, a little louche.

As he broadcast his carefully crafted life story, no doubt well-rehearsed, she gave the occasional unenthusiastic 'hmm' of ascent and remembered again why she had chosen Patrick.

"So, how about you?" he eventually asked.

As if you actually care.

"GP conference in London," her brusque response.

Raised eyebrows.

Clearly underestimated me. Not just a pretty face then.

"A doctor, wow."

May just as well say "Good for you! Clever girl!" Patronising jerk.

"Yes, I'm a doctor. For my sins."

It felt sooooo good to say that.

"So where do you practise? Devon? Cornwall? Not Exeter, I hope," he added with an exaggerated grimace.

"Nope, you're safe there. But I'm in even more of a backwater in Devon. Deep in the shire. I love it ."

"Yep, horses for courses," he conceded, hands up in surrender.

Emma didn't really feel much like hearing more of the same about him and so offered a little more of herself.

"I moved from London ten years ago. Best thing I ever did, to be honest. A great place to bring up my daughter. Plenty on our doorstep to distract her from screens. She's actually never happier than when she's outdoors, on the beach, in the woods, running around on the moors."

"How old is she?"

"Nearly nine."

"I've got an eight year old and a six year old. Always on screens. Not that I have much say in it, they live with their mother. If I had my way with them, it'd be a whole different story."

Divorcee on the pull. Know-it-all dad.

Emma simply smiled and hmmed.

"How about you?"

"How about me?" she teased.

"Divorced, single?"

Cut to the chase. So, he noticed the lack of a ring.

Intrigued by where this conversation was heading, the woman on the table opposite shifted a little in her seat, stealing a glance at Emma.

Emma held his gaze, "I live with my partner. He's Alice's dad."

Breaking eye contact, he lowered his gaze just a fraction. And then, straight back at her, "Been together long? What does he do?"

Determining the pecking order.

Clearly trying to establish the lie of the land.

"Patrick teaches, primary school, part-time. It's a great job for working around Alice. My job can be all-consuming at times."

Raising his gaze and misjudging the situation, the silver fox reclaimed his Alpha male mantle and introduced himself somewhat ceremoniously.

"Well, it's really nice to meet you, I'm James." His firm handshake across the table, holding hers just a beat too long.

Chapter Two - Emma

Withdrawing her hand, "Emma."

James continued talking about himself as the train headed up through Tiverton Parkway and on to Taunton. Laying out his wares, promoting his brand.

Again, Emma reflected on her life with Patrick. Rooted, caring, kind, dependable Patrick. The more she listened to James prattle on, the more grateful for Patrick she felt. Secure in who he was, Patrick never felt the need to preen, to puff himself up. A slight guilt crept in for considering flirting with the silver fox.

But hey, I'm only human.

Coming into Taunton, the train manager once again apologised for the late running of the train. The woman opposite started to assemble her belongings and wriggle into her coat; her onboard entertainment cut short.

Emma seized the moment and shifted the dynamic. "Well, time's getting on. I'd better check a few emails." Turning her attention to her laptop screen, she added, "No rest for the wicked, eh?"

She may not have relished the one-sided conversation, but she couldn't help but feel a slight frisson from the attention James had paid her.

Guilty as charged, M'lud.

James smiled, deflating slightly, and settled back in his seat, checking his phone. Eyes down. Fingers tapping and swiping.

The rain, still relentless, streaked down begrimed windows; the view partially obscured. Deciduous dieback had left skeletal trees; leaden skies their portentous backdrop. The outlook was bleak.

At Taunton, a group of bedraggled passengers boarded their First Class carriage. Rain-smacked faces and dripping coats, two of them made their way to the table opposite Emma and James. Emma noticed how James watched the younger of the women peel off her coat, overtly appraising what she revealed.

She felt indignant. Indignant that his eye roved so quickly. Indignant on behalf of the woman so obviously being pored over. Indignant with herself.

I'm such a hypocrite. I love the attention. I hate the attention. I want it on my terms.

As she scanned her emails, she thought of Alice. Funny, rambunctious, intrepid Alice. Almost nine, rapidly approaching adolescence. How much longer would her daughter be so delightfully straightforward, so unselfconscious, body confident, secure in her own skin? How long had she got before puberty, peer pressure and angst entered the picture? She feared for her.

Patrick and Emma had consciously chosen to give their daughter everything they could to equip her for her future. They were providing her with a holistic, wholesome upbringing in the countryside; parenting her together as a team; and going all out to present her with positive role models. Values, aims and objectives bound Patrick and Emma tightly together as they fashioned their family life.

And yet, Emma still shuddered when she thought of all that Alice must face as she navigated through her adolescent years into adulthood. Few came through unscathed.

For Patrick, it was scars of rejection. An absent mother. An overworked and emotionally deficient father. His mother had left when he was five, leaving him rudderless for his childhood and adolescence. His memories of her little more than shadows.

Chapter Two - Emma

Cushioned and cocooned in a loving family environment herself, for Emma it was forging her medical career that had later left its scars.

Patrick's wounds were deep, and she loved him all the more for them. Hers, by contrast, felt more superficial. And yet, they still smarted. Casual sexism, gender bias, lack of respect, inappropriate behaviour - she'd encountered it all and more. Whilst she had got on well with the majority of her male cohorts and colleagues, some of whom were now her friends, a significant minority had been a real issue for her. It wasn't only the dinosaurs; it was also her peers. Carving out her career had not been without its snags and stumbling blocks. Maintaining her career was not without its struggles.

Her dreams for Alice were that she would rise, that she would fly unfettered. Her experience tempered her dreams.

For Alice to fly, she would have shackles to shake off, hurdles to overcome and ceilings to break through.

Plus ça change.

Breaking into her brooding, the trolley steward drew up alongside them, offering lunchtime refreshment. Emma ordered a cup of tea and selected a sandwich from the limited range. Not the most appetising sandwich she had ever had, but she was in need of some sustenance ahead of the onward push across the city. Her stomach would thank her.

James took the opportunity to make it a lunch break for them both, making small talk around her choice of sandwich and his. She noted, with distaste, that he spoke with his mouthful. Not the best look with a BLT.

Careful what you wish for.

She began to really rue him sitting down at her table. Pre-empting another tedious one-sided conversation, she surrendered a little more of herself.

"Yes, not my lunch of choice but the train's running late, and I need to scoot across on the Elizabeth line to ExCel. There won't be time to stop off anywhere for lunch. I want to catch an afternoon lecture and workshop before checking into my hotel later. It will be all go when I get there."

Both women opposite shot her a look.

"Off to the RCGP?" the older one enquired.

"Yes, I am." A slight dread creeping over her.

"So are we. We're based in the same surgery in Wellington. We're staying at the Novotel. Where do you practise?"

Caught off guard, and not wishing to engage in a parallel conversation, Emma's smile was forced.

"South Devon," her somewhat frosty reply. She repositioned herself so as to firmly face James.

The lesser of two evils.

"So, James, tell me about your kids. Do you get to see them much now you're on your own? I expect you miss them."

Giving James the field, she settled back into her seat as he waxed lyrical about his paternal attributes and the genius and prowess of his offspring. Deflection successful.

Patrick would have laughed. Half of his Year 3 were alleged geniuses.

As the train wended its way towards Reading, Emma resigned herself to James's conversational conceit. Complaints about his ex-wife, anecdotes about the child prodigies, and tales of his own gallantry were interspersed

Chapter Two - Emma

with the occasional question about her life, scant attention paid to the replies.

The women in the seats opposite had quickly turned their attention back to their own conversation; chewing the fat, cooking up plans for the days ahead.

Probably think I'm a cold fish.

Today was not the day to get chatting to doctors on trains. She would have plenty of opportunity to connect and network with her own kind at the conference, should she choose to. Her train journey was something separate. Set apart. Her own mise-en-scène.

James wasn't exactly her first choice for the starring role, but at least he wasn't a medic.

And so, the train and their unequally coupled conversation rolled on and on until Reading. As the pace slowed and they crept towards the station, the train manager proudly proclaimed that the train to London Paddington, having made up for lost time, was now on course for a timely arrival.

Small mercies.

James, pausing for breath, diverted his attention to the tightly packed platform, granting Emma an opportunity to take out her phone and intently check her messages.

No sooner had the Reading bound contingent alighted, a fresh wave of passengers flooded the train; those joining First Class transformed the atmosphere with their citybound drive and metropolitan vibe. A palpable sense of purpose pervaded the carriage.

Emma determined to give herself headspace for the final stage of her journey into the capital. Busying herself with laptop and phone, she focused her eyes on her screens but released her mind to drift. A picture of purpose. A portrayal of productivity. A perfect sham. Taking the hint, James fell silent.

Time slipped past and the train gathered pace once more, pushing out of the suburbs and into the city. It arrived, as promised, on time at Paddington Station.

Mission accomplished. Well done, Emma.

Emma wished James a polite and pointed farewell as they both gathered belongings, pulled on raincoats, and prepared their exit. If he'd been harbouring notions of swapping numbers, she had roundly dashed his hopes. Their connection had run its course.

Leaving him in her wake and stepping off the train, she had the sensation of shedding a skin as she joined the throng on its push and shove to the ticket barrier. Out the other side, she was propelled into the mass and tangle of travellers; lives to be lived, stories to be told. Each weaving a way ahead, creating their own web. Spinning their own yarn.

Picking her way across Paddington's crowded concourse, Emma soon arrived at the confluence of mainline and underground. Veering off and preparing to descend into the depths of London's subterranean network, she began to mentally gear herself up for the days ahead.

Paths to be crossed; connections to be made; tales to be told.

Chapter Three
Amelia

The best way to predict your future is to create it.

—Abraham Lincoln

Spent, Amelia stared at her reflection long and hard in the washroom mirror. She needed this time to recover some inner strength, to reset herself. It was another one of those relentlessly wet, mizzly November days when clothes soaked, hair frizzed, glasses fogged, moods dampened, and tempers frayed. An arduous couple of days, followed by the inevitable battle through the five o'clock crush and rush, deep in the bowels of the suffocating Northern and Bakerloo Lines, had left her feeling chewed up and spat out. Surfacing at Paddington, she had breathed a long and deep, appreciative sigh of relief. She had finally crossed into new territory; a province in which she could divest herself of the trials of the previous days.

The harsh, unflattering light of the washroom in the First Class Lounge at Paddington did nothing to lift her spirits. Her savagely-lit mirror image highlighted the gossamer threads tracing creeping patterns around her eyes and the corners of her mouth. Unwelcome brassy tones streaked through her rich copper hair. Her skin sallow.

Who designs these places? Sadists?

Down but not out, Amelia touched up her make-up, restyled her hair into a sleek low bun, and made up her mind to make the most of her journey back home. Time to destress, decompress, digress.

Prawn salad and a can of G & T from Marks or Pullman dining?

She plumped for the Pullman. A more substantial meal and company for distraction would do her good. A reward, or compensation. Within the confines of the Pullman carriage, a microcosm of privileged lives, she could recast herself, regenerate.

With less than an hour before boarding, she wouldn't be able to book in advance, but she was confident that she could smooth-talk the Pullman Dining Manager to squeeze her in. There was always some availability on the 19.04 from Paddington to Plymouth. The only fly in the ointment would be if she didn't get a forward-facing seat. She'd sooner forgo dinner than feel nauseous travelling. Chances were that a fellow traveller would swap with her. Worst case scenario, alcohol and snacks in First Class.

First World problems.

Leaving the washroom, Amelia checked the information board and saw that her train should be departing on time but was not yet ready to board. She probably had a good twenty minutes to sit and recalibrate. Shunning, as was her wont, the modern, somewhat sterile front lounge, Amelia made her way to the octagonal rotunda: Queen Victoria's waiting room, no less. The period features and softer chandelier lighting lent a certain gravitas to her travel experience; an inner sanctum far from the madding crowds. Ensconcing herself in one of the wingback Chesterfield armchairs, with her hastily grabbed coffee and copy of The Financial Times, she surreptitiously surveyed the room.

Chapter Three Amelia

A typical Thursday evening clientele; a panoply of business suits, polished shoes, tailored dresses, silk blouses, and high heels. She blended right in. No cheap weekenders with their jeans, jumpers and Skechers.

A duo sat apart: a different breed, conspicuous in their attire. Both women were dressed up: the blond one uber-glam, the mousy brown one understated. They were drinking prosecco, the blond one loudly holding court.

Amelia was drawn to them, wanting to know more about who they were and their particular dynamic. Having a very limited set of close friends herself, she was always intrigued by what made other people's friendships tick. Tuning in, she could pick up snippets of conversation which drifted across from the loud blond.

"Oh Jen, you really shouldn't bother, she's not worth the effort."

"I simply don't see why you don't ..."

"... you should get bloody George to do it. He's their dad, Jen ..."

Judgements, opinions, and Prosecco were flowing.

Amelia's intrusion was cut short when the Mouse suddenly got up, grabbed her bags, and informed her friend that their train was ready for boarding on Platform 8. Looking at the information board, Amelia saw they were travelling on the same train as her, and it was, indeed, ready.

The First Class Lounge sprang to life as the majority of its transients gathered coats, luggage and travel paraphernalia and set off in the direction of Platform 8. Amelia quickened her pace and headed straight for the Pullman, determined to dine.

No smooth talking necessary, there were a few spaces left, and Amelia had the choice of two tables: one with two middle-aged, middle-spreading men in suits - ties, and jackets now gratefully shed; the other with Blondie, the Mouse and one other woman. Two of the available seats faced forward.

No contest, this could be interesting.

"I'll take the table with the other women, please," she informed the Dining Manager and made her way into the carriage.

Having removed her coat, stowed her bag in the overhead rack, and noticed both men turn, indiscreetly, to check her out, she took her seat, greeting her dining companions with a warm and open smile.

Reel them in.

"What a miserable evening," she ventured. "It's so good to be on the train at last."

Mouse smiled, about to respond, when Blondie cut in, "Total nightmare weather. What do you expect in November though? Bloody miserable, as always. You going far?"

"Totnes," Amelia replied, "I live a short drive from the station. How about you?"

"Jen and I get off in Exeter. Jen changes for Barnstaple there, don't you Jen? I live in Exeter."

Jen nodded in agreement.

Is Jen mute? Let the woman get a word in edgeways, for crying out loud.

Before Blondie could continue, the other woman, who was sitting opposite Amelia, chipped in, "I'm on until Exeter too. I'm —"

"Well," interjected Blondie, "this should be jolly. We've just been on one of my 40th birthday breaks and we're not ready to wind down just yet. Who's up for wine?"

Amelia and her counterpart opposite shared a look, an unspoken judgement. Both agreed to the wine.

Chapter Three Amelia

"I'm Melissa, never Mel by the way, and this is my oldest friend, Jen. Not literally. Same age. Just we've known each other since secondary school, haven't we, Jen?"

"Jennifer," Jen asserted, sotto voce.

Not mute.

"Ros," Amelia's opposite number added.

"Amelia."

As the train pulled out of the station, Amelia inwardly decompressed. Relinquishing the pressures of her brief sojourn in London, she relaxed into this new space; the next stage.

The women didn't have long to wait to order drinks, and Melissa was quick to ask for a bottle of Sauvignon Blanc, ostensibly without consulting her friend.

"You're welcome to share," she offered the others.

"Actually, I'm a red girl myself," Ros countered.

"Snap," Amelia concurred. This wasn't strictly true. "Shall we share a bottle, you choose," she added.

"Great, if you're sure," said Ros, turning to the waiter, " A bottle of the Rioja, please."

"Certainly, Madam."

As the waiter left to fetch the wine, Amelia commented to the others, "I love this dining service, but I do hate being called Madam. Makes me feel about eighty-four."

The others laughed their agreement. Each of the women was around the forty mark, give or take a year. And bang on for Melissa. A generation caught between Madam and 'hey gurl'.

As the train pushed on out west through the dark November night, their little enclave began to adopt the convivial common bond of the shared Pullman experience.

Amelia held back somewhat: evaluating the players; gauging the interplay.

Melissa was the more outwardly dominant of her three dining companions. She was also the most striking, not necessarily for all the right reasons. She was slim and pretty with long poker straight, platinum blond hair. Highly decorated, with over-plucked brows, lending her an unfortunate look of constant surprise, long bright talons, emblazoned designer labels and pumped and plumped up lips, she somehow managed to look a little indecorous.

More money than style.

Jennifer, by comparison, was dressed down whilst clearly having dressed up. Her whole demeanour, from head to toe, was less varnished, less enhanced, and yet there was something of quiet quality about her.

Loyal. Long suffering.

Ros, the wildcard, was tall and handsome. Her thick ash blonde hair cut into a sleek bob. Minimal make-up on an open, fine-boned face. Ros carried herself well, with an air of quiet confidence. Amelia imagined she was a thinker; a lot going on behind the cool gaze of her steel grey eyes.

I like her.

Breaching Amelia's internal, not altogether kind, appraisal of her present company, the waiter brought the wine and was ready to take orders for starters and mains.

"Oh great, wine. Sorry, we've not got round to deciding on food yet. Give us a few minutes," Melissa instructed.

"Of course, Madam," pouring wine.

Wry smiles all round.

Chapter Three Amelia

Wine poured; the four women sat in silence contemplating a West Country themed fine dining menu. By the time the waiter returned, they had all decided on their starters and mains. Amelia felt suddenly ravenous. A suppressed appetite over the past few days had left her feeling hollowed out.

Better get something down me before this wine goes straight to my head.

Orders in, conversation resumed.

"Oh, good for you Jen, going for the tortellini followed by the steak. Treat yourself, we're still celebrating. It's good to relax your diet, rein it in again next week, eh? I wish I could be so relaxed," Melissa observed.

Oooh meow. Cat and Mouse.

Jennifer blushed, suddenly self-conscious of her choice of meal.

Probably needs comfort food, poor little Mouse.

Ros shot Amelia a look, eyebrows slightly raised, a brief flash of contempt evident. Amelia knew they were most definitely on the same wavelength.

Hackles rising, Amelia threw Melissa a momentary look of disdain before addressing Jennifer directly, "So, are you forty already, Jennifer? Or were you born after Mel? Same school year, I know." She was careful to shorten her name.

Melissa winced ever so slightly; her left eye twitching. Ros suppressed a satisfied smirk.

"Not until next June. Mind you, Melissa isn't forty until March. She's just starting the celebrations early, aren't you Melissa?"

Recovering quickly, "Hell, yes. Making the most of it while I can! My husband's an Officer in the Royal Marines. We've travelled all over, but he's based in

Lympstone training recruits at the moment. It means that I get to settle for a bit and catch up with some old friends. Been great hasn't it, Jenny Jen?"

Jennifer smiled in magnanimous agreement.

Too sweet for your own good, Jenny Jen. Toughen up buttercup.

"And we've both got three year olds which is lovely as we can meet up with them. And Jen's other three, if we have to, in the school holidays! Full house with you Jen, isn't it?" Melissa laughed.

"Wow, four kids. Must be great to have a bit of a breather," Ros suggested.

Not sure how much of a breather she's actually had.

"Well, it is but I'll be glad to get back to them all too," Jennifer replied, a little wistfully.

Starters arrived as Melissa marvelled over Jen's heroic parenting of such a boisterous tribe, when she found it hard enough with just her little Billy, otherwise known as her "little Billy Boo Boo".

Did your brains turn to mush along with your birth canal? Stupid cow.

Amelia caught herself.

What is happening to me? I am becoming snide, bitchy. Must be hangry. Time to eat. Keep it sweet.

Amelia's tastebuds sprang to life with the first mouthful of tender scallop: buttery, briny and slightly sweet. Melt-in-the-mouth marshmallows of the deep. She savoured the sensation, eating slowly in spite of the urge to bolt all three of them down. The meanness she had felt creeping into her spirit started to dissipate. The potency of food, the power of gratification - however fleeting; hanger temporarily placated.

Chapter Three Amelia

As wine continued to flow between the first two courses, tongues began to loosen a little more.

Managing quite deftly to cut into Melissa's tales of life as a Royal Marine wife and a slightly 'I know I don't look it' older first-time mother, Amelia enquired of Ros the reason for her trip to London.

"Work," Ros explained," I'm a German Lecturer at Exeter Uni and I was attending a meeting with one of my counterparts at UCL."

A thinker. Sie ist natürlich eine Denkerin.

Resurrecting her A Level German.

"How interesting. I bet that's a great job and a beautiful place to work too. I loved languages at school. Thought I might study them further at one time."

"Oh, what stopped you?"

"Too caught up with dreams and visions, schemes, and plans. Got sidetracked really. Business degree instead. One day maybe I'll pick up the thread again. Who knows?"

"So how about you?" Jennifer asked Amelia, clearly complicit in steering the conversation away further from Melissa's dominance. "What have you been to London for?"

Clearly not mute, and clearly not blind to her friend's toxic traits. Long suffering, nonetheless.

"Business. I run a number of small businesses, and I was checking in with one of my London based teams."

Before she was required to elaborate further, dinner was served: Dover sole for Amelia, Ros, and Melissa; prime West Country fillet steak for Jennifer.

"You clearly made a good choice there, Jennifer. Looks delicious," Ros enthused.

I love Ros.

They continued talking and sharing what they cared to reveal of their lives as they tackled their main course: Jennifer audibly savouring the steak; Ameila trying to quell hunger pangs without greedily wolfing down her food; Ros meticulously cutting and chewing each small mouthful; and Melissa picking at her plateful whilst knocking back her wine and ordering another bottle.

Eats like a bird, drinks like a fish.

As the train rolled on through the darkness, dinner was eaten, wine flowed, stories were told, plates were cleared, dessert was refused by all four, and coffees were ordered.

Amelia loved travelling after dark. There was something exhilarating about speeding through the night; darkened skies lending an air of mystery and glamour to the otherwise banal setting of the Pullman carriage. Glancing at her reflection in the train window, she imagined she was watching a version of herself in a play. The glamourisation of a mundane scene; the mystique and romance of the night shrouding the banality of the everyday. A flight of fancy.

As their coffees arrived, Melissa and Jennifer were occupied messaging husbands, checking on children, and giving their ETAs. As if by an unspoken agreement, Ros and Amelia uncoupled themselves from the two friends, leaning into one another and embarking on their own exclusive tête-à-tête.

"So, Amelia, I'm intrigued. You shunned languages for business. Tell me how you got into business, and what sort of business?" Ros asked.

"Long story, I've always been a bit of an entrepreneur, I guess. My mum would say I was a dreamer, my dad called me his little hustler. We didn't have much growing

Chapter Three Amelia

up and I knew I wanted more; not just materially, but experience-wise too. My parents were great, and they were happy together, but I wanted more from my life than they seemed to have. I'm more driven than either of them ever was. I worked hard to get to uni and then studied for my business degree, whilst launching various start-ups, some successful, some a flop. It took a while to get to where I am now. I suppose I saw making money as a means to finding experience and adventure."

"So, have you found them? Experience? Adventure?"

She's a real thinker, this one. A prober. Need to keep on my toes.

"Well, there's a question. My life has been pretty eventful, I suppose. Not always in the ways I imagined it would be. And my businesses have done very well. Dad always said I could sell coals to Newcastle. I would be that kid flogging toys and books outside the house; busking badly on the high street - more concerned about the coins than the chords; nagging the neighbours to pay me to walk their dog or clean their car; and going through all the lockers at the leisure centre for coins left in the slot. I saw it all as initiative. I can even remember mum asking me to play my guitar for grandad and me putting a hat out on the kitchen floor for him to pay me. And I wasn't even any good. I was a pushy madam." She caught herself and laughed, "There's that word again!"

Ros laughed, "I can imagine you were rather persuasive."

Amelia knew this to be true. Some might say persuasive. Others said, forceful, demanding. Amelia had always been determined, driven. The adrenaline rush experienced pursuing an idea, chasing a dream, and realising a vision was second to none. Scheming, plotting, twisting, turning, pushing, pulling. She was a woman in perpetual motion. Onwards, upwards. Always looking ahead. Never looking back.

"So, what exactly is it you deal in?" Ros drilled down, wanting more.

"Oh, I have a finger in lots of pies."

"I wouldn't expect anything less," Ros grinned.

"Mainly health and beauty, recycling initiatives, sustainable fashion. How about you? You must have a pretty full-on work life?" Amelia steered the conversation away from her work, keen not to dominate, anxious not to give too much of herself away.

"Yes, it can be pretty demanding. Juggling it with a husband and young children is the hardest part. Never enough hours in the week."

"How old are your children?"

Ros talked at some length about her son, Finn, who was twelve, her daughter, Orla, who was nine and her husband Liam, of indeterminate age. Her cool grey gaze softened as she spoke of them. A pretty close-knit family by all accounts. A tightly woven clan.

"And you? Family?"

"No kids. Recently single, divorced."

Amelia caught one of the men opposite chance a furtive glance.

Dream on Casanova. Single, not desperate.

"Oh, hope you're through the worst of it. Not an easy time, I expect."

"Well, I'm gloriously child-free and single now. Not too bad from my vantage point," Amelia responded, careful to sound just a little exultant, but not an outright bitch.

Chapter Three Amelia

"There is certainly something to be said for that, I'm sure."

"Well, yes for me, at any rate. I was married for ten years, and I'd been clear from the get-go that kids were never on the menu. Greg was fine with that, or so I thought. I'm simply not mother material. Other people's kids are fine, I just don't want my own. I think Greg thought that I'd mellow, that the proverbial biological clock would start ticking. Only it never did, and I wasn't about to wind it up."

"And he couldn't accept that?"

"Not really. Our marriage was good until the penny dropped for him and then it just became more and more of a battleground. That was until I decided to retreat and wave the white flag of surrender. I gave up my marriage rather than give up my conviction. Not over sharing, am I? " she laughed softly.

"No, not at all. I love hearing other people's stories."

Join the club.

"Sad though," Ros continued, "I feel sad for you, and sad for him that he didn't take you seriously in the first place," Ros empathised.

"Well, it was a bit of a relief for both of us in the end, I suppose. He has moved out, moved on, and is happily expecting his first child with a more amenable partner. It's pretty amicable now."

Melissa and Jennifer sat back, ears cocked and fingers tapping as they messaged and scrolled, both clearly earwigging on the current revelation; a trace of disdain clouding Melissa's face, a hint of admiration flickering across Jennifer's. Ros simply listened, nodding her understanding.

It feels so good to be the exception to the rule: to say I am an entrepreneur, I am child-free, I am divorced. It feels good to be set apart; to feel like a somebody, a someone else.

An automated announcement heralded the imminent arrival of the train into Taunton.

"Taunton already," Amelia echoed.

Nearly two hours down and only one to go before it's all change again.

As the train crept into the station, Amelia gazed through the window. The relentless rain had still not abated and the two people leaving her carriage had shrugged on raincoats and were poised, umbrellas at the ready. Lending the platform an ethereal, almost supernatural quality, misty rain formed light pillars and auras. Ghostly figures, hooded and hunched, awaited the arrival of the train, keen to cross the threshold from spectral to corporeal. Alighting passengers, making space for their passage, ventured out into the dark enchantment of the night.

"Just look at that weather," Ros sighed. "Not looking forward to that at Exeter."

Melissa seized upon the opportunity to segue into the conversation, "Oh I know, I'll be glad to get home and tucked up in bed. Shame for you Jen, you need to change for Barnstaple."

"Yes, probably be on a boneshaker at this time of night. I'll be glad to get home too."

Tête-à-tête well and truly cracked open, the four women returned to their contrived camaraderie. Rebinding their temporary ties, platitudinous exchanges shuttled back and forth for the last half an hour before Exeter St David's; each woman, in her own way,

Chapter Three Amelia

retracting the stopgap intimacy of their shared journey. By the time coats had been wriggled into, handbags and luggage assembled, and the perfunctory faux heartfelt farewells made, Amelia felt a growing sense of relief welling up within. Whilst she had enjoyed, needed even, the distraction, she was grateful for the time and space for her mind to switch track before her arrival at Totnes.

Released, Amelia acknowledged to herself that she was pleased to shake off the lives of others; lives she wouldn't want to be tethered to. Not even to Ros, who she had liked. Mentally relishing her own carefully crafted persona as a newly single, child-free, fully focused career woman, she congratulated herself for stepping away from her former identity as wife, worker, and potential child-bearer. She had successfully exchanged a precarious existence balancing the needs of a spouse with her own to find more solid ground. It hadn't been easy, it hadn't always been pretty, but she alone would now have control over her own destiny; the joy of creating her own future. Unencumbered, she had reclaimed herself.

And yet ....

A whisper of misgiving. An uninvited flicker of foreboding. She didn't feel entirely sure-footed.

Arriving at her destination, Amelia composed herself once more. Stepping out of her manufactured milieu, she knew she must adapt again for the challenges ahead. Challenges of the workaday world.

Life may be what you make it but, if experience had taught her anything, it wasn't always predictable.

Chapter Four
Eva

Our value lies in what we are and what we have been, not in our ability to recite the recent past.

—Homer

There is no greater journey than the one travelled by the mind. In the course of her sixty-four years on the planet, Eva's mind had journeyed far and wide: her imagination a labyrinthine adventure. She had always been an enquirer, a quester, a dreamer: her mind in constant flux, its fertile landscape well-watered, its roads well-travelled.

On a cold, bright late autumn day eight years ago the terra firma of Eva's life had suddenly given way. Perched on the edge of her seat in the consultant's sparsely furnished office, the hard and cold fact of her diagnosis had hit her like an earthquake, pitching her from solid ground into a wild and stormy sea. As she remained seated, hand-in-hand with her daughter, all that she had feared, and pushed to the very recesses of her mind, became her reality. Life thereafter continued on a precarious trajectory: her slow decline bestrewn with aftershocks. As she later entered increasingly hostile terrain, control of the mind she once prized slipped further and further out of her grasp. A crushing sadness, a piercing grief would come over Eva in her more lucid moments. It was as if she were trying to clutch water: its

Chapter Four - Eva

steady stream slipping through her fingers, its life-giving force just out of reach.

In recent weeks, Eva had found herself increasingly pulled back into distant memories; strands of a life once lived weaving their way into her present reality. At times, they felt more than memories as they pushed their way from her past into her present: a rebirthing of a bygone existence. Shifts in time brought hope, then confusion, as moments of love and life lifted her spirits, only to depart just as suddenly as they appeared. Her vision blurred; her identity obscured.

Sometimes, catching sight of herself in the mirror, she would not recognise the woman staring back at her: wiry steel grey tendrils hijacking burnished copper hair; a deeply furrowed brow; purple thread veins conspicuous through paper-thin skin; a lacklustre gaze.

Where am I? Who is this imposter?

Eva's life now well and truly adrift, memories alone tendered a temporary anchor. They broke through pell-mell, neither rhyme nor reason dictating their course. Her brain wandered back and forth, crossing time zones: her life a jumble of disjointed scenarios. The vagaries of her mind pitching her this way and that.

Eva as lover, besotted, audacious. She had loved deeply, hopelessly. She had met her lover in the dog days of the summer of '83: temperatures soared, the heat was sultry, their affair torrid. Head turned, heart swollen, soul laid bare, Eva had chosen to overlook the ties binding her lover to another life. Her mind now revisited his passionate kiss; his tender embrace; her deep yearning; his urgent, ravenous lovemaking; their rapture. Joy coursed through her ravaged mind: love reawakened, hope rekindled. She was the wide-eyed, infatuated woman of her youth once more, holding him and holding her secret: the child within her, not yet visible, not yet revealed. Eva as mother. Eva as lover.

Eva as grandmother, doting, capable. Her mind propelled her back to a railway journey from Paddington Station to the West Country. Armed with sweets and treats; colouring books and felt-tip pens; Bob the Builder jigsaw puzzles; and a head full of plans, Eva was fully prepared for the days ahead. Tasked with single-handedly caring for her young grandsons whilst her daughter and son-in-law jetted off to Budapest for a mini-break, Eva knew she needed to have all bases covered. She adored her grandsons; they added light and life to her world. She had always looked forward to time spent with them, but she now knew what a handful young boys could be. Having raised a dreamy, somewhat introspective daughter, these boys were something of an eye-opener for her. She would need to be on her mettle, ready to engage, set to swing into action. She must ensure she was well-fortified and well-rewarded. A gin or two of an evening would definitely help. Relaxing into her memory, a faraway look in her eyes, Eva sat gazing out of the train window, watching the urban landscape retreating as the busy train forged ahead, pushing further and further out of the metropolis. She looked forward to seeing her daughter, her grandsons, her son-in-law even. She was buoyant. She was self-assured. She was unshakable. Eva as mother. Eva as mother-in-law. Eva as grandmother.

Eva as Evie, headstrong, tenacious. Launched back to a particularly warm and sunny spring day at school in 1968, she tore around the playground, laughing, caterwauling, caught up in flights of fancy and make-believe. All of a sudden, she was flying through the air:

Chapter Four - Eva

arms flailing, crashing to the ground, face planting, lip splitting, arm breaking. Teachers rushed, children screamed, her best friend Lizzie stood stunned and sobbing. Eva is, once more, tough little Evie: biting her lip, forcing back tears, chin up, colour drained, stouthearted. In her mind's eye, she is comforting Lizzie, reassuring teachers as they await the arrival of the ambulance. Her mind sharpens, her heart swells, pride rises. Eva as warrior. Eva as friend. Eva as Evie.

Eva as mother of the bride, devoted, disquieted. Whisked back to the sumptuous surroundings of the exclusive North London hotel, Eva is sat deep in thought, outwardly celebrating, inwardly grieving just a little. The wedding reception is impeccably tasteful, the bride beautiful, the groom debonair, the future bright. And yet, Eva was unable to shake off an insidious sense of misgiving. As her new son-in-law spoke at length of his deep love for and undying devotion to his Titian treasure, the woman of his dreams, Eva prayed inwardly that her daughter would not lose her own sparkle, her own vision. Aware reality would inevitably bite, she willed her daughter to hold fast to her identity, to cling onto her own dreams and desires and become the mistress of her own destiny. Eva as champion. Eva as protector. Eva as mother of the bride.

Eva as single mother, abandoned, resolute. Divorced from the present, her mind now inhabiting a Friday afternoon in the late '80s as she finished her shift and gathered her thoughts before setting off to pick her daughter up from school. She is excited, anxious to get there on time as they will be collecting a kitten for her fifth birthday. Suddenly, her far-flung reality breached, an unfamiliar voice startled her, "Hi mum, it's me Penelope, your daughter."

Careful to announce her arrival, deliberately reminding her mother of her name and her connection, Penelope settled down in the armchair opposite Eva. In regular contact with the care home manager, Penelope had been fully briefed that her mother was now showing signs of rapid deterioration. Shifting in and out of time zones and places, sometimes repeatedly in the course of a day, Eva's behaviour had recently become more erratic, her care more challenging.

Eva stared, a blank expression, "What do you want?" she demanded.

"It's me mum, your daughter, Penelope."

Eva sneered, "Liar. Bitch." Her face contorted and she looked ready to spit.

Eva lost at sea. Eva now.

Forcing herself to remain calm and divert her mother, Penelope spoke gently, "Would you like me to get you a drink? I'm just off to get one for myself. Shall I get us a nice cup of tea?"

Rising slowly from her chair, Penelope was poised, ready to call for help. No need, her strategy had worked; Eva had visibly simmered down.

Meltdown deftly averted, Eva retreated from the now into her hitherto world, "No time, I need to get Penelope from school. It's her birthday."

"Oh, how lovely. That's special. How old is she?"

"Five, I'm getting her a kitten." Eva's face lit up, brimming over with love and light.

Mirabelle. Scratchy, mewling ball of fluff. How I loved that cat. How I loved mum for buying her.

Tears pricked Penelope's eyes. Loves lost.

Chapter Four - Eva

Eva tried to rise from her chair, looking around her, "Where's my coat, my bag? I have to go, I'll be late." Confusion was etched on her face, as her arms stiffly refused to propel her up and out of the chair.

"It's fine, you still have time. Shall I get that tea? You've got time for a quick drink, haven't you?"

Eva looked directly at Penelope, perplexed, searching her face for clues.

Who is this woman? What does she want?

"Okay," she agreed, keen to get rid of her. "I need to find my bag."

Giving her mother time and space, Penelope decided to take a short walk in the grounds. Eva could wait a while for the tea, she would forget anyway. Penelope reflected on the changes in her mother over the past couple of years since she had moved into the specialist care home. It was a good home, as far as they went. Money was no object for Penelope, and she had ensured that her mother had everything she could possibly need, materially at least. It had been a particularly tough time for Eva and for Penelope, and not just because Eva had entered the later stages of early-onset Alzheimer's.

Barely settled in the home, the pandemic had struck, rocking their world and the world at large. Already grappling with transition anxiety and the shifts in pace and routine, both Eva and Penelope had now faced a whole host of extra pressures: fear of COVID itself; visits suspended, then contained and curtailed; isolation; despondency. Eva's confusion redoubled. Life would never be the same for either of them and they could never reclaim the time they had missed together, but, on this particular visit, Penelope was thankful; she was now, at least, fully present with Eva, albeit Eva could not reciprocate. Memories of greeting her confused mother through a window and in a sterile tent still haunted Penelope; unbidden images of the disorientation and distress vividly painted across her mother's ashen face would assail her in the dead of night.

As she walked back to the home to fetch tea for her mother, she resolved to make the most of the very precious little time she had left with her, whatever that may look like. The time to grieve would come soon enough. For now, every moment was an opportunity to enter Eva's world and journey with her, however rough the ride might be.

Re-entering the resident's lounge, Penelope made her way to the far corner where her mother sat slack-mouthed, staring blankly out of the large Victorian oriel window.

"Mum, it's me, Penelope. I've brought tea. It's just how you like it, mum. No sugar, lots of milk."

Eva turned towards her daughter, her shaky hand reaching for the beaker. She was calmer now, docile even. As she sipped tea from the spout, she eyed her daughter: recognition flickered, a loose connection was made.

Seizing an opportunity, Penelope reached slowly across and took her mother's free hand in her own, gently caressing it. Eva relaxed back into the armchair, a warmth rising from somewhere deep within her. Sat hand-in-hand with this stranger, she experienced a familiar attachment: the muscle memory of her heart triumphing over the decline of her mind.

As reality receded, love survived in Eva's heart, in her soul, in her very spirit. For whom, she could not always recall and yet, right now, searching for answers in the piercing green eyes of this young woman opposite her, she felt a rush of tenderness. Tears trickled down her face. Imprinted in a deeper place, love would always win.

Eva loves. Eva is loved. Eva now.

Chapter Five
Tori

I will wear my heart upon my sleeve
For daws to peck at

—*William Shakespeare, Othello*

Arriving at the railway station intentionally ahead of schedule, Tori had been for a half an hour walk before seeking respite from the cold in the Signal Box Café. It had been the perfect opportunity for her to stretch her legs and clear her mind ahead of the long journey upcountry to London. Having parked up and navigated the temperamental parking app, she had set off along the riverside path, gladly embracing the brief hiatus between car and train. Drinking in lungfuls of reinvigorating early morning air, she had managed to shake off the last vestiges of sleepiness and grogginess from too little sleep and too much red wine the night before. The bracing air had roused and quickened her senses: her misty breath, a visible reminder of life yet to be lived.

Carpe diem.

Glacial overnight temperatures had left their spectacular imprint on the riverscape. The bleak beauty of white-tipped trees, frost-bitten bushes, and swirling spirals of mist over the River Dart infused Tori with a sense of well-being. Whilst her extremities had felt the pinch, her spirit had expanded, and her energy levels had

Chapter Five – Tori

started to rise. Peace reigned. Hope rose. All was well in Tori's world. For now.

Returning to the station, chilled to the bone, Tori headed for the popular greasy spoon, perched above Platform 2. Tentatively pulling back the door, she was greeted by wafts of sizzling bacon and the warm smile of the woman taking down orders and taking up payments at the counter. A regular traveller from this station, she had never before ventured into this well-loved bolthole. It was just after 8 o'clock on a frosty Friday morning in December, and she was surprised to see that this little corner of the town was already a hive of activity. It was a great contrast to the early morning somnolence of the High Street itself, where you were pushed to find a shop or café open before 10am.

Behind the counter, a bevy of bustling women were busily cooking up countless plates of full English for those nestled at tables, whilst simultaneously doling out bacon baps and sausage sandwiches to those preparing for flight. The clientele was a peculiar pastiche of men in heavy-duty winter work gear and hi-viz jackets; executives and white collar workers in suits and office wear; and others, like Tori, who couldn't be so readily pigeonholed, muffled up in mufti. Some were clearly part-way through their working day already, others were preparing for the long haul ahead.

A frequenter of vegetarian bistros, vegan cafés, and trendy plant-based eateries, Tori was not in her natural habitat. Whilst she felt a little out of her comfort zone, she was very grateful for a hot drink and somewhere to sit as she waited for the 08.42 to Paddington. Enveloped in the warm, fuggy atmosphere of the station café, her frost-pinched ears and nose started to thaw. Her hands, circling a large mug of steaming tea, acted as a conduit channelling heat, her body slowly starting to defrost. Settling back into her seat, sipping slowly, Tori allowed her mind to roam freely, oscillating between events of the past week and plans for the long weekend break ahead.

After twenty minutes or so absorbed in contemplation whilst reanimating her frozen form, Tori suddenly craved fresh air again. The strong smell of fat and pervasive fug had started to clog her nostrils and seep into her hair and skin. What had initially felt warm and welcoming now felt cloying and claustrophobic. It was definitely time to decamp.

Descending the short flight of steps from the Signal Box to the platform, Tori surveyed the scene and was very glad of her seat reservation. Packed with late commuters, college students, Christmas shoppers, and long weekenders, the platform was not easy to navigate. Picking her way through the huddling hoards, she found her boarding zone and composed herself for the short wait.

There was still a little time to feel the sharp, exhilarating bite of the winter morning and imbibe its crisp, fresh air. Skulking low in the sky, the pale sun was desperately seeking to break through; a few hours more and it would become a welcome friend bearing a surprise gift; winter rays would permeate exposed skin, radiating into bone and marrow, caressing even the darkest of souls. Tori raised her face towards it, inviting even just the most fleeting of touches, a cursory kiss, an embrace before boarding.

Later, hunkered down in her seat, her coat a blanket over her knees and her chunky knitted snood a cushion, Tori messaged the group chat:

Chapter Five – Tori

En route, can't wait to see you all. ETA Paddington 11.29.

This was mostly true.

Tori's train was due in at 11.29, and she was en route. She turned her thoughts to her friends from vet school, Jo, Rachel, Sarah, Emily, and Esme. She was very much looking forward to catching up with four of them. Overbearing Esme, not so much. There would be lots to talk about, and she was especially keen to catch up with Rachel, as she too specialised in avian vet services. Whilst Tori's area of expertise focused on the care and treatment of pet birds, Rachel's field was poultry management. They affectionately called one another 'Little Bird' and 'Big Bird'. There would be so much to talk about with Rachel, and so much to learn. Rachel would have had her work well and truly cut out for her, assisting with biosecurity and flock management during this latest outbreak of avian flu. Catching herself, Tori recalled that this weekend was primarily an opportunity for fun.

All work and no play clips my wings.

Each of Tori's friends, busy with careers, relationships, and, for some, children, needed a break. Their annual get-together was sacrosanct: a hallowed interstice in their crowded lives. Each woman, released from her own particular gilded cage, eagerly seized the moment. It was time to ruffle their feathers, spread their wings, fly free.

Tori's mind was abuzz with messages and emojis pinging back and forth:

Can't wait.

Watch out, Hampstead.

Soon be cocktails o'clock.

Running late, be there by 3.

Spa booking confirmed for this evening, make sure you're waxed and polished girls!

Trust you, Jo.

Messages fabricated; expectation building. Tori's mind was running away with her. Glancing at her screensaver and stashing her phone in her handbag, she was keen to digitally detox and mentally escape awhile.

One thing Tori loved about a train journey was the golden opportunity of a conversation with a stranger: a brief encounter. She would be captivated by glimpses into the lives of others, imagining their experiences and recreating their stories. Many of her transitory connections had been inspiring, enchanting even. The things people opened up about on a long train journey together never ceased to amaze her; the temporary intimacy between two people, never to be resumed, could be tender, poignant, romantic even. Her partner, Rob, dismissed it as just simply being a nosy parker.

No chance of a brief encounter right now.

The young girl sat alongside her in the aisle seat had studiously shielded herself from the real world; Beats headphones firmly clamped on, Samsung Galaxy in hand, she was lost in music and Snapchat. She wasn't surfacing anytime soon.

Probably off to Exeter College.

Tori consoled herself with the fact that the seat was booked from Exeter to Reading.

Still a chance to be a nosy parker.

Turning her attention to the magical winter landscape beyond the grimy window, she soaked up the shifting scenes. The train pushed on through rime-frosted fields before yielding to the expansive coastal landscape

Chapter Five – Tori

beyond Newton Abbot. A true thalassophile, Tori's spirits always soared as she approached the stretch from Teignmouth to Starcross. This morning didn't disappoint; a grey green sea, as flat as a millpond, spread itself out extravagantly, lavishly: its meeting point with the steel grey sky barely perceptible. The sea was so calm and so still that the horizon resembled a distant precipice. Tori could almost appreciate the spurious logic of the flat-earthers; it was as if by sailing too far, you could fall off the edge into who knows what, and who knows where.

And who could really know what lies out there beyond the extent of our perception?

What wonders, what sights, what experiences?

Tori's life had been carefully mapped out and heavily scheduled: school, gap year, university, veterinary practice, partner, house, parakeets, dogs: a well-ordered, fully functioning, productive existence. She sometimes wondered what would happen if she deviated off course, if she dared voyage into the unknown. Popping in and out of the red sandstone tunnels, it felt as if she were being offered tantalising glimpses of possibility beyond the constraints of her mind. Seascapes and mindscapes.

Garish carbuncular buildings, blots on the Dawlish landscape, rudely pulled her back into reality.

Why, oh why, do we always get it so wrong?

A lover of the sea, Tori was no lover of your typical seaside town; tacky arcades, grubby gift shops, gaudy diners, and rundown amusement parks always made her feel a little despondent. Man's ability to spoil God-given beauty, to create an eyesore out of something once so eye-catching, somehow made her think of reality TV stars.

Averting her gaze, Tori opted to fix her eyes purely on the view out to sea until the train reached Starcross. She loved this stretch: deer spotting at Powderham Castle, and bird spotting on the estuary approach to Exeter. At this time of year, she would be on the lookout for the waders who made these flatlands their winter home. She had taken out her binoculars in preparation and was able to pick out a number of them from among the scattered colonies of gulls: stocky oystercatchers, their red-orange bills vivid; striking, elegant avocets, their slim bills snootily curled-up; and a lone curlew, its sickle-shaped bill, comically oversized. Each bird a beauty, a distinct miracle of creation. Leaving the delights of the natural world in its wake, the steel wheels of the train propelled it on to Devon's capital city.

The young girl next to her emerging from her virtual reality, rolling up a cigarette, and gathering her belongings in preparation for re-entry into the physical world, Tori chanced a quick glance at her phone. Thirteen unread messages, one from home. Twelve could wait. She pinged back a short reply to the message from home and re-stashed her phone.

Stationed awhile at St David's, the carriage emptied considerably before being restocked with a whole new batch of chilly, hand-rubbing, foot-stamping travellers; all seemed keen to find seats, plump down and thaw out. One such incomer, kyphotic, weather-beaten and badly combed-over, squinted at a number of overhead reservations before struggling out of his overcoat, and lurching rather forcefully into the seat next to Tori.

Well-dressed. Fairly affluent. Late sixties. Arthritic. Maybe got a tale or two to tell. Worth a shot.

Chapter Five – Tori

Tori smiled politely in welcome. He smiled back, revealing a large wad of food caught between his bottom incisors. Controlling herself outwardly, she winced inwardly and refrained from pointing it out; social decorum sadly preventing her from enlightening him and soothing herself. They journeyed alongside one another in silence until the drinks trolley drew alongside; he gallantly deferred to her as orders were taken. Tori thanked him.

"Tea, please. White, no sugar."

"Anything else with that, Madam?"

A shake of the head, a bright smile, and a tap of her bank card.

"Sir?"

"Coffee, milk, two sugars. That's all," he barked.

As the trolley host moved listlessly on to the next sale, Barker stirred milk and sugar into his coffee and fished a Tupperware box from his string bag. Painstakingly smoothing and laying a cloth napkin on the tray table, he placed a generous wedge of homemade fruit cake squarely in the middle of it. He then set about breaking off chunks and eating them with great gusto. It did look rather good.

Obliging wife. More tooth debris. Hopefully, the coffee will flush it out.

"Much better than the standard train fare," he yipped, suddenly.

Tori had to agree, "Yes, it looks delicious. Homemade, I presume."

"Yes, wife's a top cook. Can't fault her. Great fruitcakes. Top cook," his rat-a-tat style of speaking reminded Tori of an old friend of her father's: an Army Colonel, replete with medals, brimful of himself.

Stifling a snigger and overlooking his patronising attitude, Tori decided to take up the conversational baton; this could be entertaining,

"I see you're off to Reading. Any nice plans for the weekend?"

"I'm on my way to a reunion," he explained. "Visiting some old naval friends. Wife gives me time off for good behaviour sometimes. Life in the old sailor yet," he guffawed at his own jokes.

"Oh, that's lovely," Tori replied, "I'm actually on my way to a reunion myself. I'm meeting my old university friends in London. We try to get together once a year. Obviously, it's been a bit hit and miss the last couple of years. How about you?"

"Not as often as you do, every few years, I suppose. Depends who is available, and who's still alive," he snorted. "Leaving hubby at home then? Lovely young lass like you must be married?"

Cringe.

"No, I'm not married. I have a partner."

"Of course, old-fashioned of me to presume. Lucky chap. Good to have time apart, though. Absence makes the heart grow fonder and all that. Better watch out though, while the cat's away," Barker chortled. Full of presumptions, full of clichés.

I'll have a little fun with him.

"Well, I'll definitely be having a good time. My partner, on the other hand, has a list of jobs to do after parkrun tomorrow morning."

"Parkrun, eh?" Barker bellowed. "Good on him. Love a parkrun. Can't do it since the old knees have given out, but I take the lab for a jaunt in the woods, whilst my wife runs it. She's pretty fast and she's determined. It's in

Chapter Five – Tori

her blood. Mind you, it's not about competition, is it? All about the camaraderie and bonhomie. That's what I love about it, no judgement, no pressure, open to all." He barely paused for breath.

Must be pretty fit for her age, or a darn sight younger than him.

Tori feigned unreserved agreement. A regular runner herself, she had witnessed wars of words over dog harnesses giving an unfair advantage; sly, smug smiles over results and coffee; and passive-aggressive buggy pushers vying for poll positions.

"Both my daughters run regularly," he continued apace, whilst manoeuvring a large chunk of glacé cherry out of his back teeth. Tori averted her gaze, feeling a little queasy.

"Pips is a natural sprinter. Ran for the county when she was younger. But she loves a parkrun. Minty's not quite so fast, but she's not far behind in the rankings. And the stamina of a horse, that one. Was even running at seven months preggers."

Barker was blissfully unaware of the irony of his words.

So much for no judgement, and no competition.

Mischief bubbled up from somewhere deep within.

"Yes, I know, it's great that it is so inclusive, isn't it? Rob loves it even though it is more of a parkhobble than a parkrun since losing three toes last year. We've had real problems trying to find the right trainers since the accident."

Barker was temporarily thrown off-guard, fumbling the conversational baton, before quickly recovering with, "That must have been hard. How did that happen? Poor chap!"

Mischief simmered.

"Well, long story really; it was a rather bizarre accident at work. Wrong place and wrong time. It was pretty gruesome as they were ripped right off. It's probably best not to go into details. I wouldn't like to put you off your coffee and cake."

"How bloody awful. Good for him, though. Still running. Top job. Yes, good fellow."

Mischief came to the boil.

"Good for her, yes. Rob's short for Roberta."

Barker visibly dropped the conversational baton like a hot potato and shuffled awkwardly in his seat, as he processed the revelation that he was sitting next to a lesbian whose girlfriend hobbled around parkrun with only seven of her ten toes remaining. He smiled stiffly, sipped his coffee, mumbled a gender-neutral, "Good on them" and took out his newspaper. The conversation had clearly run its course. Tori took out her vanity mirror, tucked loose copper strands of hair back behind her ears, smoothed her brows, and reapplied her lipstick, pointedly.

That felt so good. Pretty little liar. Who's the poor chap, now?

Tori could not wait to share her latest brief encounter with her friends over cocktails. And with Rob later, of course. He would, no doubt, laugh, and then tell her, once again, that she was becoming a rather prolific liar. Her friends would all squeal with tipsy delight. Jo would be outwardly and loudly outraged, but privately unsurprised, having experienced so much prejudice, on so many levels, on grounds of her sexuality. Jo had developed a thick skin and a robust attitude since coming out in her early twenties. Tori admired her fortitude.

Chapter Five – Tori

To thine own self be true.

Of late, Tori had developed a habit of tweaking the truth for effect, to divert, or to impress. She wasn't exactly sure when this had started, or why. Rob had gently teased her to start with, but now it had become a running joke. Whilst her frequent fibbing made for a funny story or an amusing anecdote, it also unsettled her at times. There were lies that were seen and lies that were unseen; at times she was hidden in plain sight. The kick she got out of pulling a fast one, telling a porky, or even inventing a whole scenario would, on occasion, knock her off balance. It was as if each fabrication tipped the carefully calibrated scales of her mind a little further, unbalancing her mental equilibrium. Somewhere deep inside a warning bell was signalling a slippery slope ahead. She wilfully chose to ignore the signs.

Oblivious to the web spun around him, Barker perused The Times, his spectacles perched precariously on his aquiline nose. Tori had turned her mind's eye to the hitherto neglected group chat, skimming multiple messages, bestowing appropriate emojis, and giving a quick sitrep before disengaging and burrowing into her seat for a snooze.

Train on time so far. See you all later. Wait until you hear about my latest train lark! Time for a snooze! Winky, smiley and sleeping face emojis.

Tori could never really sleep on trains, but closing her eyes and resting her busy mind was always a pleasant way to kill time. As the train pressed on upcountry, she retreated into herself, imagining her happy state, her secret space, her dreamscape. She daren't share this fantasy, not even with Rob, for fear that in naming it, it would fly forever out of reach. Gradually, her breathing started to slow, her heart rate dropped, her jaw slackened, and her muscles started to unclench. Relaxation was, however, fairly short-lived.

Brakes squealing, bodies jolting, the London bound train came to an abrupt standstill, somewhere in the boondocks west of Reading.

No drama. We'll be off again soon. Breathe in, breathe out. Relax.

Mutterings over spilt coffee, heads raised from books and devices, exaggerated sighs, and the noxious smell of brake dust.

Nothing serious. Breathe in, breathe out.

Until fairly recently, Tori had not given enclosed spaces a second thought. She had been a frequent flyer, a habitual train traveller, a nonchalant lift passenger. However she travelled, Tori would passively surrender control, go with the flow. The mechanics, logistics and trajectory of the ride were of no concern to her, as long as she reached her destination in one piece.

Tempora mutantur.

Information was not immediately forthcoming. Passengers sat in ignorance for a good ten minutes: restless, tetchy, indifferent, resigned, re-immersed in books and devices; each had their own way of handling the delay. In spite of herself, Tori could feel a small panic rise within. The sealed windows and locked doors, which did not trouble her when the train was in motion, now started to oppress and stifle her. Battling her mind, and harnessing her breathing as best she could, she resisted the urge to stand up and move out of her seat to seek her own answers. She quelled the desire to cry out and make a scene. Doing nothing, hearing nothing, was almost unbearable.

Chapter Five – Tori

What is happening to me? Why do I feel so out of control?

Barker came to the rescue with a timely distraction.

"Bloody trains. Wouldn't have happened back in the day. Even bloody British Rail ran on time, didn't stop for every bloody leaf on the track, and they bloody well let you know what was going on." Barker was bloody annoyed. Tori was bloody grateful for his opinionated interruption of her unnerving introspection. And also, just a tad sorry for spinning him a yarn: a yarn within a tapestry.

As if in an attempt to appease Barker, the train manager's voice crackled over the intercom, "Good morning again, Ladies and Gentlemen. We are very sorry for the sudden halt and the delay to this service to London Paddington. We have been informed of a signal fault just outside Reading. We hope that this will be rectified within the next half an hour. Again, we apologise for the delay and will update you as soon as we have further details."

Knowledge is power.

Tori regained some control over her addled mind with the realisation that the delay was not entirely without a timescale, and that someone, somewhere was in control. The carriage felt a little more spacious, the air a little more breathable.

She resolved to build bridges with Barker by offering him an extra strong mint, which he gratefully and lip-smackingly accepted.

"Don't mind if I do."

Penance.

After a little chit-chat, Tori excused herself and, to keep her mind fully in the present, scrolled the news on her phone. Conversation and occupation served to distract her and take her beyond the confines of the capsule in which she was confined.

Within half an hour, and after a couple of updates from the train manager, the train had started, to Tori's great relief, to venture forward. No longer stuck, both physically and mentally, she was able to regain a little more inner composure.

Another episode to unpick with my psychotherapist later.

But for now, returning to the core of who she really was, she brooded. Reflecting on her physical and emotional responses, both within her current frame of mind, and within its wider framework, she felt unsettled. Reluctantly she had to concede that, in spite of its excitement and gratification, fantasy was now negatively impacting her everyday reality. The further she strayed from truth, the more she invented, the more her mind fractured. She was birthing fictions, only to leave them to die; a part of her always left behind. Her indulgence, far from freeing her, had left her trailing a broken wing.

And yet, she could not, would not stop. Not just yet.

Chapter Six
Ella

*The most painful thing is losing yourself in the process
of loving someone too much,
and forgetting that you are special too.*

—Ernest Hemingway

Squinting out of one sleep-sticky eye, she peered furtively from under the duvet. He was shifting from one foot to the other, trying his best not to wake her, as he struggled into his trousers in the dead of night darkness of an unfamiliar hotel room. Once he had satisfied himself that he was adequately attired to leave the room, he chanced a quick glance back at her, before creeping towards the door: shoes, jacket, and phone in hand. She re-clamped her eye and murmured lightly, feigning slumber. A click of the door and he was gone.

Rolling over, she reached for her phone to check the time, 2.22am. The wee hours of the morning: in more ways than one the older she got, she thought wryly.

Starfishing across the sumptuous King Size bed, she felt a sense of rising power, laced with a hazy scent of danger. She felt wide-awake and fully alive. Figuratively and literally undercover, she basked in her conquest.

Suddenly ravenous, she rose and dialled room service. Another advantage of her wealth, she could afford to stay in the most exclusive of London hotels: the staff at your beck and call, whatever the hour.

"Oh, hello. I'd like room service, please. Belgian waffles with blueberries. And hot chocolate, with cream. Room 608."

"Of course, Madam, anything else I can help you with?"

"No, that'll be all."

"We'll be with you in around 15 minutes, Madam."

"Perfect. Thank you."

She replaced the receiver and hopped out of bed to go to the bathroom, weighing her options before deciding against a quick shower. That could wait until the morning proper. For now, she could still imbibe him: the trailing scent he had left, an olfactory reminder of her allure, their chemistry, the alchemy of the evening before. She had no desire to wash that off just yet. Instead, she wrapped herself in the fluffy hotel robe, cleansed her face, and brushed out her tangled hair. Scrutinising her reflection in the mirror, there was something she didn't quite recognise in the familiar physiognomy of the woman meeting her green-eyed gaze. This night had been a watershed moment for her: one from which she could not easily turn back. A line had been crossed; a choice had been made. The essence of who she had once been, was no longer reflected back at her. Within the carapace, a different creature had made her home.

Following a gentle tap on the door, the ceremonious delivery of night-time treats, and a generous tip, she sat alone, relishing her forbidden fruit. The woman she once was would never have indulged in midnight carbs, milky drinks, and sex with a stranger. Tucking into the feast set before her, she allowed her mind to revisit the events and delectation of the night before, savouring each detail.

Chapter Six – Ella

She had arrived at the hotel later than originally planned on a sub-zero January evening. Her train had been delayed again. No surprise there. The countless strikes of the summer, autumn and winter had almost become the norm, and she no longer expected to arrive at a planned destination at the right time, or even on the right day. On this occasion, she was only an hour later than scheduled. Not bad considering the weather. There was still plenty of time to make the most of the hotel facilities and seek out an adventure before the demanding days which, no doubt, lay ahead.

January: a new year, a new start, a new me.

The Christmas period had been tough, but she had set her face like flint to embrace the year ahead. Changing direction again, she would live it to the full. She was on the lookout for possibilities. She was open to suggestions.

Having checked in, freshened up, restyled her hair, and changed into a figure-hugging dress and kitten heels, she had been almost ready to brave the hotel bar before dinner. A sweep of Rouge Allure across her lipstick-ready puckered mouth, a dab of Coco Mademoiselle behind the ears, condoms in her handbag; she was well and truly good to go.

Her first foray into the unknown world of pick-ups and hook-ups, she was ready for anything, even to fall flat on her face. It had been years, decades even since she had thought about putting herself out there. There hadn't been the need, or the desire.

Outwardly, she knew she still looked good for her age: poised, chic, confident. Inwardly, she had to suppress gnawing doubts and squirming fears, whilst silencing the negative voices which would often plague her. She had reassured herself, reminding herself that she was in a safe space, had exit strategies, and really had nothing to prove to anyone.

Except maybe myself.

Quickly, resolutely, she had shut down that particular thought.

She had stayed in this hotel, albeit under entirely different circumstances, on a handful of occasions over the last twenty years, and she felt secure in the knowledge that it was high-end and discreet. This establishment would, naturally, only broker a certain clientele. Whilst she had not exactly been searching out a one-night stand on her previous sojourns, she had seen enough to know that the hotel bar would be well-stocked with corporate high-flyers. Off the leash, some would undoubtedly be amenable to a night's diversion from high stress jobs and high maintenance wives. Champing at the bit even.

Finding her way to the bar had been easy, and she had hoped the next phase would be just as straightforward. Her memory had served her correctly, and the room was awash with just the right sort of man: her prey.

Positioning herself at the far end of the bar, a G & T at her fingertips and her legs crossed elegantly as she perched on the bar stool, she had lain in wait. She had deliberately left any hide-behind props in the room. No phone, no laptop, no book. She had wanted to be fully present, fully available. She had given herself half an hour until her dinner reservation, enough time to settle her nerves with an aperitif, enough space for an approach.

As she surveyed the room, weighing her options, she felt a new wave of energy flood through her veins. The thrill of the chase.

In her former life, she had always been the prey, never the hunter. The scales were tipping, the tables turning.

Chapter Six - Ella

Surveying the room, she had picked out a number of options: the big game. She also ruled out many more: the turkeys. She was up for a fling, but she still had standards.

And suddenly, there he was. Just ten minutes or so after her arrival, he had entered the bar. From first glance, she knew he was the one: the contender, her conquest.

He was tall, very tall, 6'5 at a guess, broad-shouldered, jet black hair and slightly louche. She scented blood.

He approached the bar, stood near to her, but not too close. She could see him appraising her out of the corner of his eye.

"Laphroaig on the rocks, make it a double." His tone was commanding, his accent Home Counties, his demeanour assured. The bartender set about preparing the drink as her appraiser took his position on the bar stool next to her.

She felt a stirring from deep within; a wave of excitement swept her body, tinged with a ripple of nausea.

What am I doing here? It's not too late to back out.

Thanking the bartender, he shifted a little on the bar stool, his body angled just a little more towards her. She noticed the quality of his shoes: calf leather Oxfords if she wasn't mistaken.

Am I actually doing this?

"Oh, that's good. I needed that."

Having taken a slug of whisky, he addressed his comment to no-one in particular, and yet, glancing her way, clearly gave her an in. She noticed his intense blue eyes and long dark lashes. No wedding band.

What the hell, I'm doing this.

Trying desperately not to clear her throat audibly, even though she was afraid she may sound hoarse, or worse still, squeaky with nerves, she managed a, "Hard day?"

"Hard week," he said.
"Well, nothing a stiff drink can't remedy, I hope."
"We'll see."
We will.
Slowly moving in for the kill, "So, are you working here in London?"
Purposefully turning himself on the bar stool to fully face her, "Yes, I'm here on business. I'm actually based in the States. California. You?"
Perfect.
"I'm here on business, too. Based in Devon, not quite as exotic!"
"A lovely part of the world though. What do you do?" he replied warmly.
"I'm a solicitor. Corporate law. You?"
"Wealth management."
"Plenty of that to manage in California, I expect."
"Indeed, there is. I'm based in Manhattan Beach. I get to come back from time to time though, best of both worlds."
"Sounds perfect."
"Yes, it can be a little lonely at times though. Lots of travelling, lots of hotel bars."
"That must be pretty hard on your family," she ventured.
"I'm divorced, no kids. No-one to care about it."
"Sorry, I presumed."
"Hey, don't apologise. I'm happily divorced and happily childless," he smiled. "Does that make me a little unsavoury?"
Not in the least.
She laughed, looking at him from under her perfectly groomed brows and volume-enhanced lashes.

Chapter Six - Ella

Lure him in.

"Well, in that case, I'm about to have dinner. Fancy joining me? I could do with some company."

He baulked, ever so slightly, before taking her up on her offer.

Clearly used to being the hunter.

"Yes, why not? That'll be lovely. I'm Gabe, by the way. Gabriel, but only to my mother."

A good upper middle class name.

"Ella."

She didn't tell him that, breaking free from the bonds of her working-class roots, she'd rebranded herself as Ella at University. Danni just wouldn't have cut the mustard at Chester Law School.

Hands were shaken. Deals were done.

Having rejigged their dinner reservations, they had taken their places opposite one another in a cosy corner of the hotel bar. He had ordered another double whisky on the rocks for good measure. She had chosen sparkling water, keen to pace her alcohol intake and keep her mind clear, her focus sharp. As they perused the menu, choosing their wine, starters, and mains, she stole the occasional glance at him, pinching herself under the table.

Is this real? Am I really doing this? Is this really me?

After they had ordered, he had excused himself.

"Nature calls. I'll be right back."

As he walked across the dining room, she saw him pull his phone from his pocket, look at it, touch the screen, and place it against his ear.

Calling home? Maybe not so unfettered?

There was something in the way he carried himself which led her to doubt his projected persona. If she was right, he was in good company.

He had returned quite quickly, and resettled himself, turning his full attention on her.

Over starters, baby squid paired with a glass of unoaked Chardonnay for her, Cumbrian beef tartare paired with a glass of Barolo for him, they launched their gameplay, swapping scripts.

He told her about his recent divorce from Manon, of how she had left him and returned home to France, citing his poor work-life balance as a reason to bail. He knew she was lying and had reconnected with an old flame, an ex-amant. He had admitted that he didn't have a leg to stand on, his work had indeed devoured him whole, leaving only crumbs of his presence behind.

"Do you have any regrets?" she probed, courteous rather than curious. She had no concern for his actual wellbeing.

"Not really, as I said before, I am happily divorced. I was with Manon for ten years, the passion had long gone. For her as well as for me."

"And yet, it's lonely at times?"

"At times, yes. A little. But I can always find a worthy distraction."

He had looked directly into her eyes as he spoke. Brazenly, she had held his gaze, determined not to be the first to look away.

I win.

He had lifted his wine glass, raised it, proposed a toast, "Here's to an evening of distraction."

As she clinked his glass, she felt a flush creep up her neck. She knocked back a generous gulp of Chardonnay, and then reached for her handbag, before excusing herself to visit the washroom.

Chapter Six - Ella

Her bladder and her feet had thanked her as she released both in the privacy of the toilet cubicle. The kitten heels might do wonders for her calves, but they were crippling her feet. She would need to kick them off under the table.

Taking her time in the washroom, she had allowed the cold water from the tap to course freely over her wrists, cooling her off both physically and mentally. Revisiting her story in her mind, she recollected herself before returning, as cool as a cucumber, to their table.

The remains of the starter had been cleared away, and she noticed Gabe had ordered a bottle of Pinot Noir. They had both ordered the pan-seared filet mignon, rare. He knew his wine. He also knew how to regain control.

"I hope you don't mind, I ordered for us. Are you happy with the Pinot? It pairs so well with the filet mignon," he asked, not really giving room for dissent.

"Perfect. My choice every time," her short, clear reply masking the dichotomy within: irritation at his presumption paired with an earthy excitement with tones of titillation.

During the main course, the focus gradually shifted from Gabe's profile to Ella's.

He had admitted that he had noticed her earlier in reception as she was checking in. He had come out of the lift just as she was filling out her paperwork.

"You caught my eye. I have a thing for redheads," he smiled mischievously, as he leant over the table and touched her hand. "I had hoped to see you later."

Sounds familiar.

Chewing slowly, she savoured the soft, sweetness of the steak before running her stockinged foot slowly up his leg, and replying, "And I hope you haven't been disappointed."

"Au contraire."

She had then shared something of herself: her recent separation from her husband of fifteen years, his growing desire for children, her disinterest in procreation, and her repugnance at the thought of pregnancy.

"When all was said and done, I wasn't going to ruin my body or mind for children. Owen accepted that, but I knew that resentment might build. Besides, I was ready for new experiences. Does that make me a little unsavoury?" she teased.

He laughed and topped up her wine.

What she had failed to disclose was the wider contexts occupying her fractured mind. She was unwilling to unpack the downward spirals which led to the separation.

Ella had loved Owen deeply and passionately, just not unconditionally. She wasn't an idiot, but she had been naive. She had yearned to be everything to him and for him: an object of desire and a promise of fulfilment. In the early days, this had been their truth. They were so wrapped up in one another that nothing else mattered. They lived, they worked, they loved. Life was good. They had sworn everlasting love to one another alone. Eyes, bodies, minds were exclusively theirs: unencumbered, unsullied. And yet, with the years that passed, something had shifted. Owen had wanted more, and not just children. He had started to hanker after new experiences, new friends, new women.

Ella was no longer enough.

Her shock at this realisation had slowly morphed into fear and then a deep resentment. She had loved him so much, too much, and when that love was no longer

Chapter Six – Ella

enough for him, she had felt undermined, displaced, rejected.

This shift in their dynamic was something she would never have foreseen. She could not comprehend why Owen would want to destabilise their relationship, and why he was so intent on derailing them.

She had indeed had a choice to make but it hadn't been that straightforward. She had suffered, she still suffered. She had cut Owen loose before he could entangle her in his mess. But it was not a clean cut. Bitter threads of resentment and rejection wound their way around her heart.

There's a fine line between love and hate.

Owen had not loved her enough and for that she could not forgive him. Her recovery, her revenge depended on her ability to reinvent herself, live life on her terms, and take what she could with no strings attached. She had changed. Pure and simple love had been contaminated. She was a different animal.

Steak, washed down with wine, and fictions swapped, it had been evident to both players that dessert would be skipped. There was clearly only one bonne bouche left on their menu.

He had chivalrously offered to settle the bill. She had refused. Her desire to take charge, to dominate, had been a driving force.

"I invited you. Let me pay," she had insisted.

"No way. Absolutely not," he had retaliated.

They had reluctantly compromised and split the bill: each feeling a fleeting loss of power.

This battle for dominance had, however, translated well into the hotel bedroom, leading to highly-charged sex. The excitement she had felt with him had reawakened something deep within, long suppressed. Like animals, they had both taken what they needed until they lay spent, exhausted, satiated.

Her long-held fantasy of sex with a stranger had crossed over the threshold of her mind, breaching it, and crashing full-force into her reality. Revisiting the details, she felt as though she were peering vicariously into the lives of others.

Eventually, having replayed the most sensual and erotic scenes a number of times in her mind, she endeavoured to sleep, knowing she needed to recover some strength. Dozing fitfully, she drifted in and out of sleep, at times unable to distinguish between her dreams and actuality.

Her iPhone's alarm pulling her out of her halftone world, she dragged herself out of bed and took a long, hot shower, washing off any residual scent of him and the tell-tale traces of their entanglement. Even as she scrubbed, the heady rapture of the night before was already starting to dissipate. Reconnecting with herself, she had begun to feel just a little sullied, adulterated even. The more she scrubbed, the less clean she felt. Some things can't be expunged.

A new day was dawning. She needed to refocus, redress herself.

As she dried off, remade her face, and got ready for the day ahead, she quickly quelled any pangs of regret. Leaving the hotel room, beautifully attired and adorned, she mentally patched over the gaping tear in the fabric of her being.

And yet, the bona fide woman secreted within, could feel the stitches straining, the patch pulling.

Chapter Seven
Husband

*How blunt are all the arrows of thy quiver
in comparison with those of guilt.*

— *Robert Blair*

A creeping dread spread over him as he boarded the Penzance bound 14.04 train from London Paddington, the prospect of returning home looming like a dark shadow clouding his horizon. His shoulders were slumped and his back ached: physical reminders of the carnal acrobatics of the previous evening and the guilt he bore. He was travelling alone. He was nothing if not discreet.

Having found his seat and smiled a cursory greeting to the couple opposite, he took out his laptop, phone and reading glasses. As he messaged his wife, informing her of his scheduled arrival time, he was particularly careful to express how much he was looking forward to being home with her and their boys. This wasn't an outright lie. In fact, he was very much looking forward to catching up with both the boys who were back home from university for his upcoming birthday weekend. He had booked the family's favourite restaurant in Kingsbridge; a big-city fine dining experience on a small-town scale with well-chosen, high quality wines and seafood to die for. This would be an epicurean delight. His family deserved no less.

Until relatively recently, Reuben had been happily married and eager to see how the future would unfold now that the boys had decamped for university. This would be time for their marriage, unencumbered by the boys' relentless schedules. Aside from the monthly visit to her mother, he would finally have his wife all to himself when he was at home. And there would, of course, be the odd liaison to boot. He may be in his late fifties, but there was a lot of life in the old dog yet. And he was certainly up for learning new tricks. The future had looked promising. Until it didn't.

Things had changed. His wife was changing. He was changing.

The guilt he was shouldering was not, as one might expect, from the extra-curricular sex but from the attachment he was forming in spite of his very best intentions. This was an unwelcome and novel experience for a man who had always been able to compartmentalise his life.

Reuben had always loved his wife. It had been love at first sight. In all honesty, it was more the sight than the essence of her that he had fallen in love with. Nonetheless, he had grown to love the marrow as much as the meat. His wife possessed an ethereal quality which had beguiled him; her sensitivity, vivid imagination and childlike wonder drawing him into her world. And yet, over the past year or so, he had increasingly sensed her pulling away from him and retreating deeper into herself. This void between them had gradually widened and strained, and it was into this ever-expanding vacuum that Matilda had tumbled. She was a gift; but one he feared could now be his very own poisoned chalice. He had some difficult decisions to make if he were to survive.

In his head, Reuben knew there could be no future with Matilda. It was one thing marrying a woman half

Chapter Seven – Husband

your age when pushing forty, it was something entirely different imagining life with a woman still in her twenties when pushing sixty. Matilda was incredibly bright, wise beyond her years and downright hot, but the generation gap was simply too gaping; she had far more in common with his sons than with him. Even so, something within him craved her, clung to her, feared losing her. And it was more than simply his libido.

Having had a number of one-night stands and brief affairs during the course of his marriage, this dilemma had taken Reuben by rude surprise. As a self-made property tycoon, his lifestyle had always been peripatetic, affording him both opportunities and cover stories for his dalliances. If his wife had ever suspected, she had not let on. These were never, for him, liaisons dangereuses. Until very recently, their sex life had been good enough, and a shared commitment to their boys and family life strong enough, to cement them together as a couple. And he had never stopped loving his wife, even in the hard times.

Reuben had resolved to use this hiatus journey between his covert and overt lives to weigh his options, to formulate a plan. Something had to give. One way or another, he knew he could no longer vacillate between his two worlds without reaping serious consequences. He would lose out whatever decision he made, but procrastinating would only make the pill he must swallow more bitter.

As if aware that he would need sustenance for the journey, the First Class steward appeared with offers of refreshment. Not one to allow his emotions to suppress his appetite, he accepted a complimentary coffee, chicken wrap and slice of dry-looking fruit cake.

"Oh, and a gin and tonic. That would be great, thanks," he added to his order, hopeful that the alcohol would take the edge off the demanding deliberations he had before him.

Breaking into his world, the woman opposite asked him, "Are you off anywhere nice for the weekend? We're visiting friends in Cornwall."

Reuben groaned inwardly.

I don't need this. I really couldn't give a toss about where they are going.

Too superficially well-mannered to groan outwardly, Reuben replied, "Oh, very nice. I'm going home. I live in Devon."

Just enough to be polite.

Reuben took a very large mouthful of fajita chicken wrap.

Just enough to shut her up.

It didn't work. The woman opposite, clearly desiring diversion, and maybe, he thought to himself a little presumptuously, intrigued by him, proceeded to elaborate on their plans and ask him more questions. She didn't seem to notice or care that his mouth was now stuffed full of GWR's mushy faux Mexican fare.

Oh, for fuck's sake.

Reuben really didn't feel much like talking, especially with a mouthful of mulch, but he resigned himself to the fact that, as he ate and drank, he may as well feign some interest. He could then make an excuse to return to his own inner world: his laptop and the premise of work, a viable escape route.

For now, he went through the motions, asking all the right questions and offering just enough in response to their enquiries. All the while, Reuben was weighing up

Chapter Seven – Husband

the couple in his mind, and candidly acknowledging his own shallowness. Had this couple been more dynamic, attractive, and engaging, he would himself have been more engaged. He guessed they were a similar age to him. She was middle-aged and middle-spreading. He was middle-aged and middle-of-the-road. Reuben didn't do middling. He found the couple dull, both in appearance and personality. Had his wife been with him, she would have reprimanded him for his harsh judgements and impressed upon him that everyone had something to offer, if only you opened your eyes and truly looked. He would have conceded for her sake, whilst inwardly having none of it.

These two are boring the pants off me. Kill me now.

In an attempt to liven up the conversation, he shifted the focus on to his desire to get home and reconnect with his wife after some time away on business. He was at pains to make it clear how young she still was. He noticed Mr Middle-of-the-Road raise an eyebrow.

Jealous? What hot-blooded male wouldn't be, mate?

Reuben privately congratulated himself on his choice of wife, whilst simultaneously excusing himself for his series of escapades with younger women.

What man wouldn't prefer fresh, tender meat? Especially when it's offered up so beautifully on a plate. Poor guy with his tough mutton.

His wife would definitely have reprimanded him for those thoughts, but then he would never have shared them with her. Some things were best left unspoken in a marriage.

As the train pulled into Reading Station, Reuben flipped open his laptop and made his excuses. Opening a document, he feigned a close attention to the screen in front of him, whilst steering his mind back to the matter in hand. The decision.

What decision though?

Reuben knew there was no contest. He could not leave his wife. He loved her, and it would break her and the boys. His family would be forever changed. He had no choice. He had to end it with Matilda. The decision was not who but a whole series of hows.

How can I let Matilda down? How can I soften the blow? How can I do without her?

He was also aware that he needed, somehow, to find out what was going on with his wife and re-anchor her into their shared life.

As he thought back over recent months, he realised that his initial infatuation and then growing affection, dare he think love even, for Matilda had blinded him somewhat to the piecemeal deterioration in his wife's state of mind. It was as though he saw only a cloudy, cataract view of her. She was a fading shadow, floating in and out of his vision, never quite in focus. He needed to draw back the veil, sharpen his focus, and pinpoint what exactly was going on.

His wife had always been an enigma to him, at once both robust and fragile: her inner strength curiously coupled with inner turmoil. But she had been well for years now, and fully immersed in the day-to-day of raising their boys, her personal interests, and their social engagements. Wealth had granted her the luxury of not working, but she was always busy. He admired her for enrolling on countless courses to stretch both her mind and her body. She had always been a voracious learner, an avid reader, and a body-conscious fitness fanatic. He had always loved how she cultivated both her mind and

Chapter Seven – Husband

her body, especially her body. And yet, in recent months, he had observed her standards slip somewhat. Not only was her mind wandering, but she had also piled on a few pounds. He wasn't sure which worried him most.

As Reuben reached this particular point in his ruminations, he realised that he needed to address the enormous elephant pushed to the very back room of his mind.

Could she be ill again?

During their marriage, his wife had had two periods of what he liked to think of as unfortunate blips. He had prided himself on standing by her, paying for the very best of medical care, and getting her back on an even keel. He had done his bit. He couldn't bear to see her set adrift again; he dreaded having to pick up the pieces.

The first blip had been a real shock. His life should have looked rosy. As a recently married couple, they were still very much in the first flush of love and had just celebrated the safe birth of their boys after a problematic pregnancy. Relief and joy had flooded through them both as they welcomed their sons into the world. Financially secure, a pert nanny to help at home, and hopes and dreams of a fulfilling family life fanned out before them; they had entered their Promised Land.

And then, his wife had suddenly slipped down a very big rabbit hole. Within a week of giving birth, both her mind and body had started to dismantle. She had started to look dishevelled, slovenly even. Her rigid discipline and attention to detail had gone by the wayside. With a nanny and a cleaner, there really was no excuse to slob around the house all day. He would arrive home from work and notice, with badly concealed disgust, milky dribbles which had seeped through her nursing bra and stained the saggy loungewear she now seemed to inhabit both day and night. Her crowning glory had lost its sheen and all attempts at styling it seemed to have been relinquished. Her face was bare, but for the odd smear of who knew what. But it was not only her appearance which was going rapidly downhill, it was also her state of mind. She had always been a dreamer, a fantasist, a bit of a pretender even and he had quite liked that about her; after all, it spiced up their sex life: there was nothing like a bit of role play to get the juices flowing. But this was something else. A whole new ball game.

Suspicious, manic, and seeing and hearing things which clearly weren't there, his young wife had, at first, well and truly spooked the nanny, and then frightened him enough to call their private GP who took immediate action, admitting her and the babies to a specialist mother and baby unit. Combinations and cocktails of drugs barely taking the edge off her symptoms, the medical staff eventually resorted to electro-convulsive therapy, which mercifully restored his wife to him.

Reeling from the experience, and never wanting to witness postpartum psychosis at close quarters again, Reuben had resolved that their procreation days were over. He had been prepared to play his part in nursing his wife back to health, to pay for the very best therapists and counsellors money could buy, and to indulge her every desire but one. There would be no more children. The daughter she desired was never to be. He was done.

The second lesser blip had occurred shortly after the boys had started secondary school. Reuben had noticed that his wife was starting to daydream a little more often than usual. He was, by now, well-acquainted with her vivid imagination and her penchant for game-playing, and

Chapter Seven - Husband

he had become accustomed to her making up stories and inventing personas. On occasion, he would even play along, enjoying their conspiracy. On holiday without the boys, they would sometimes slip into different guises when meeting other couples. Artist and muse, restaurant critics, interior designers for the rich and famous, father and daughter even. Flirtations with fantasy fuelled their fun.

With the boys transitioning to their private secondary school regimes, and with more time on her hands and more space for her mind to roam, he had suspected that she was creeping slowly towards a new rabbit hole. The dreams she entertained, the games she played, and the stories she recounted were gradually becoming more frequent and more fantastical. Acting fast, he ensured his wife underwent a medication review with their GP and attended more frequent sessions with her therapist. He couldn't face his wife unravelling again. He needed her, the boys needed her. Her medication tweaked and her therapy redoubled, the second blip had been successfully controlled and curtailed.

Now, roaming alone in his own mind, he cursed himself for having been so blinkered. His tunnel-visioned focus on Matilda had resulted in him being blindsided by the encroaching disintegration of his wife. With his wife well for years, he had become complacent and had failed miserably to pick up on the tell-tale signs.

I've no choice. I have to refocus. I have to act before it's too late.

Plagued by an unfamiliar guilt, Reuben rued the fact that Matilda had fallen for him. He knew she loved, or at least thought, she loved him. She had told him on more than one occasion, and when he said it back, he more than half believed it.

Trapped in a love triangle of his own making, he felt real anguish at the prospect of edging Matilda out. Until now, he had never experienced this vein of love for a woman other than his wife. He had lusted, yes. Many, many times. But vena amoris, never. And yet within him, there was a measure of heartfelt love for his lover.

Regardless, Matilda was not the mother of his children. And, crucially, she never would be. In spite of her protestations to the contrary, Reuben knew Matilda would inevitably want her own family. He didn't buy her oh-so-modern right to a childfree life. She may choose that now but give it a few years and she'd be talking about a vasectomy reversal. Reuben would never countenance that. Not for any woman. Not only did he feel too old to sire more offspring, he had neither the need nor the desire for them. He had what he wanted: his two boys, his blood ties. And he had the mother of his boys, his marital tie. These ties bound them all together, tethering them one to another, whether they liked it or not.

Painstakingly unpicking his situation, Reuben had concluded that he must establish a workable time frame which would allow him to extricate himself from his lover with the least possible damage, whilst simultaneously recovering his wife and repairing his marriage. This would be no mean feat but, if he were to survive and thrive, he would need to disassemble one life in order to fully reconstitute the other.

By the time he approached his destination, Reuben's resolve had strengthened, and his determination to act had hardened. This particular stretch of his journey was reaching the end of the line.

Chapter Eight
Scarlett

Every man is the architect of his own fortune.

—Sallust

Scarlett picked her way through the pack of mid-morning passengers and propelled herself up the London Underground steps with undisguised relief. She never exactly enjoyed her short hop on the Tube, but this morning had been particularly unpleasant. Sandwiched between a mother with a screaming toddler in tow and a young man who had clearly failed to apply the requisite amount of deodorant, both her ears and her nose were grateful as she broke through onto the concourse at Paddington.

On drawing back the curtains in her hotel room earlier, she had been greeted by a gloriously bright, blue-sky February morning: a welcome harbinger of spring.

Typical, I'll be spending half the day on the train.

Arriving in good time at the mainline station, Scarlett spontaneously shelved her original plan to get the 11.04. Suddenly, she had no desire to head back home just yet.

And why should I? I can do what I please. I am my own boss, after all.

There were already advantages to her recent decision to walk away from the well-established architecture firm, in which she had been well-paid but understimulated for the past five years and chance her arm at self-employment.

I want more.

Brazen, and brimming over with possibilities for the day ahead, she zigzagged her way across the station to the Paddington Basin exit. She would stroll along the canal and get some fresh air; conceding, however, that fresh might be too generous an epithet for the metropolitan miasmas awaiting her.

I'll take what I can get right now.

After what had seemed like an age of leaden grey skies and all manner of rainfall variations, Scarlett was determined to seize this part of the day and soak it up before re-occupying her travelling cocoon and hiding in plain sight.

Grabbing a take-away flat white, she set off along the canal path towards Little Venice: another somewhat munificent epithet; and yet, she was always charmed by this bijou neighbourhood at the confluence of the Grand Union Canal and Regent's canals. With its Bohemian bars, funky diners, quirky cafés, and offbeat theatre venues, there was always a buzz about the place. As she sauntered slowly, dazzling February sun like gold dust on her face, her senses sizzled. Glints of light glancing off glass edifices; vividly-painted canal boats; brightly-lit underpasses; scooters speeding; bicycles breezing; varicoloured clusters of cyclamen, croci, daffodils, and primulas in canalside pots; trees heavily pregnant with buds soon to burst forth into life in all its fullness; all were reminders of life to be lived and adventures to be sought. She inhaled deeply, deliberately disregarding whatever urban toxins might be filtering down into her countryside-acclimatised lungs. She was, after all, starting to feel well and truly alive once more. And not just alive, alive and kicking. Kicking back hard.

Chapter Eight – Scarlett

World watch out.

Arriving at Little Venice, Scarlett found herself a bench overlooking Browning's Pool and settled down for a spot of people watching. An enclave of elegant Georgian houses looming large and magnificent over a kaleidoscope of colourful houseboats, her seat was positioned in the perfect spot to weigh up the omnifarious canalside comings and goings. Trendy young things hot footing it up to Camden Lock and Portobello Road; anorak-clad gongoozlers; dreamy dawdlers; waddling wildfowl; arty-farty types; and urbane dog walkers with pedigree pooches: this was, without a doubt, a bourgeois thoroughfare for those in the know. And it was right up Scarlett's street; she loved feeling both part of and separate from this genteel urban spectacle. Actor and observer, deep down Scarlett was your archetypal flâneuse.

And it was not just the people in this city-belted oasis who caught her eye and imagination: Little Venice boasted a full spectrum of architectural styles to draw her professional eye, stretch her vision, and spark ideas. In and around this exclusive West London property hotspot, period properties and state of the art contemporary design stood tall and proud; white stucco-fronted Georgian mansions, imposing Italianate villas, red brick Victorian townhouses, ornate Edwardian residences, architect-designed modern apartments, and glass creations were all vying for position.

Whilst Scarlett's work often consisted of commissions for highly conceptual modern designs, she harboured a private preference for the architecture of centuries past. In her professional life, she had to move with the market, adapt to the times, and give the client what they wanted.

But that didn't stop her dreaming and developing her own projects. One day, she may even have the time, money, and space to create her own perfectly-appointed pad.

Who knows where this venture might take me?

For Scarlett, the design of any new property hinged on the façade; the public face would always be the lynchpin of her design, setting the tone for the rest of the building, and forging its character.

You really can't beat a carefully crafted façade.

Having wiled away a good half an hour or so, Scarlett started to feel a little chilly; it was only February, after all.

Time to warm up.

Surrendering her carefully selected vantage point to a handsome older couple looking for a place to perch with their coffee and morning pastries, Scarlett made an about-turn and headed back to Paddington in search of a couple of cans of G & T and some Percy Pigs, the fizzy ones. She was feeling decadent.

And why not? Who doesn't love a Percy?

Having wound her way through the slow-footed browsers, picky purchasers and last-minute grab and goers, Scarlett secured her purchases and headed off to the First Class Lounge for a spot of primping and preening.

Senses keen, she was on the prowl. Her sights were set on an erotic happenstance; a titillating interlude; or even a fleeting flirtation would do if nothing else was on the table. Although married, Scarlett had recently cultivated a penchant for playing away. With the somewhat belated rude realisation that her husband had been sowing his oats elsewhere during the course of their marriage, she had no compunction about her own thrill-seeking. A

Chapter Eight – Scarlett

recent easy conquest had opened her eyes to new possibilities and reminded her of her own power.

What is good for the gander can be good for the goose, after all.

For Scarlett, leaving her husband was simply off the table. The product of an acrimonious divorce herself, she had sworn never to slip down that particularly tortuous spiral. With two pre-teens and appearances to maintain, she had resigned herself to playing the part of long-suffering wife and dutiful mother. But she was no martyr. She may not file for divorce, but she would take what was rightfully hers. Adventures were out there, and Scarlett had resolved to gamely grasp them, more out of a keen sense of justice than a desire for revenge. And, all the while, her nuclear family would remain intact: a carefully constructed folly. An elaborate eyecatcher.

Finishing touches to hair and make-up complete, she surveyed the end result in the washroom mirror. Satisfied with the woman she saw reflected back at her, she settled into her role. Her mantra, gently whispered under her breath, startled the woman, carefully applying her rather-too-bright and overdone lipstick, just along from her.

Keep on moving. Keep on keeping on.

"Sorry? Did you say something?"

"Oh sorry, no. Just talking to myself," Scarlett laughed, "First sign of madness, I know."

Clown Lips smiled sceptically and returned to her own camouflaging. Scarlett eyed her up and down and then left her to her endeavours, heading off to check whether her train home was ready to board. Discovering that, contrary to her expectations, it actually was, she quickly made her way to the platform, found First Class and boarded. Scanning the carriage, surveying the cargo, she took her time before settling on her sweet spot.

As she approached the table seat occupied by an attractive enough, elegantly-besuited, maybe early fifty something man, Scarlett took great care to peel off her coat, smooth down her snug-fit cashmere sweater, fastidiously flick back her hair, and slide gracefully into the seat opposite him.

He'll do for now.

She gave him her warmest smile and took out her book and phone. He returned the smile, just as warmly. As she made a show of reading messages on her phone, she was acutely, and happily, aware of his gaze hovering. She coiled a tendril of hair around her index finger, tilting her face for her very best tried and tested angle, and bided her time.

As more passengers boarded, Scarlett was willing them to sit elsewhere. This was their table. Their space. Her framed formation. She had placed her bag on the seat next to her, and she had no intention of relinquishing that seat unless explicitly required to. His raincoat was on the seat next to him. Hopefully, he would be equally inconsiderate.

Just as the carriage started to fill, and she feared she may need to surrender the seat, the departure announcement crackled out over the train's PA. The doors were soon closed, and the train departed without delay. Two huffing and puffing last minute stragglers had hurriedly boarded and quickly found their seats a couple of rows back.

Deo gratias.

They were safe.

Chapter Eight – Scarlett

Emerging from the grand wrought iron spans and cathedral-like transepts of Brunel & Wyatt's Victorian masterpiece, the station's subsequent expansions and developments respectfully drawing from and nodding to the design legacy of its forefathers, Scarlett would always feel assaulted by the perverse thrust of the train into the stark urban sprawl immediately beyond. The sprawling ugly webworks of overhead power lines, concrete cankers and architectural eyesores contrasted sharply and impudently with the magnificent, iconic backdrop. She averted her gaze, opened her novel, and waited for an opportune moment for engagement.

Scarlett had a good feeling about this one. He had potential.

As the train rolled on, further crackly announcements were made, conversations and phone calls were set in motion, and the First Class customer hosts started to make their way through the carriage, their dark Brunswick green livery a stylish throwback to a bygone era.

As the trolley approached, she accepted a tea and complimentary wrap. He did the same. Already in sync.

Should she cut the first turf? She rather hoped he would take the initiative. She was in the mood to be wooed.

"Bon appetit," his offering.

"Merci," she smiled.

"Going far?" he ventured.

"Devon. You?"

"Snap."

Cool and composed, he slowly unwrapped his wrap and prepared his tea. She noticed his slender, smooth long-fingered hands. A platinum band. She had removed her engagement and wedding rings, wearing her emerald cut ruby statement ring in their place. Nailing her colour to the mast.

"It's good to be leaving London behind for a while," he continued casually.

His nonchalance was strangely appealing, drawing her in, piquing her curiosity.

"Do you live in London, then?"

"Maida Vale."

Of course you do.

"Oh, lucky you. I love that area. In fact, I had a wander up to Little Venice before catching the train. It was a real tonic after a few days in suburbia."

"Poor you," he laughed.

He didn't ask her why or where she had been. Her appetite sharpening, Scarlett bit into her wrap and took out a can of G & T. Pulling the ring can, she decanted it into a plastic cup, caught his eye and ventured, "I have another one if you fancy wetting your whistle."

Without batting an eyelid, he accepted.

Wow, he's good.

In spite of herself, Scarlett was impressed with his mastery. She poured and proffered.

Faux clinking their plastic cups, they toasted the journey and settled into conversation; their table seats soon becoming their own distinct enclave, as they checked one another out.

She kept back the Percy Pigs. Somehow, he didn't seem the type to accept.

"I'm Scarlett," she disclosed.

"Max."

Of course, you are.

Chapter Eight – Scarlett

Anxious not to appear too eager, she let his name hang. He lounged, legs fully stretched out under the table, looking lackadaisically out of the train window.

After what seemed to her like an aeon, but, in reality, was merely a matter of minutes, Max turned his full attention on her and picked up the tempo.

"So, what takes you to Devon? Visiting? Going home?"

"I'm going home. I've been on a site visit for work this week."

"I see."

Gratified, she caught him glancing at her ring finger.

"Husband, kids?" he asked.

"Both."

"Me too. Well, wife and kids," he grinned.

His teeth were very white, very even. In fact, from his bespoke suit to his bespoke teeth, everything about him seemed made-to-measure. He was clearly a man who liked order, liked control. He definitely didn't eat Percy Pigs, she decided. Scarlett pictured herself under him and felt a hot flush of desire creep up to her neck.

"So, what takes you away from them?" she enquired.

"Oh, many things," a wry smile. "But this time, it's work."

He didn't elaborate. She didn't ask. She was rather enjoying his mystique, and she didn't want to jinx the mood with any banal revelations.

Instead, he asked about her work, her family. After waxing lyrical for some time about her passion for architecture and her foray into self-employment, she unpacked her own neatly-packaged domestic circumstances for him.

"Louis and I have been married for fifteen years now. It's become a marriage of convenience, I would say. Convenient for him, anyway," she quipped.

Phlegmatic, Max simply nodded. A cue for her to continue.

"So, it's pretty much an open marriage these days. I don't wear my rings anymore. I don't like to feel bound. We do our own thing and regroup when Barnaby and Otto are home for the holidays. Our boys are up at Blundells."

There it is. On a plate.

Her own new-found brazenness surprised her.

When did I become so forward?

She silenced a small, quiet voice, urging caution.

"Sounds like you have the best of all worlds."

Scarlett mused on his Delphic response.

The question is: Are you thinking what I'm thinking?

It was one thing being charismatic, but sometimes a girl just wanted a clear signal. A green light would enable her to forge forward, leaving any qualms and scruples in her wake.

As the train pulled into Reading, their bubble was temporarily burst with the brisk turnover of passengers. Scarlett observed, with a flutter of excitement, that he had placed his newspaper and laptop case on top of his raincoat on the seat next to him. Building up the barricade. Staking his claim.

Got him.

When the customer hosts returned with the refreshment trolley after Reading, Max presumed and ordered two G & Ts. Scarlett savoured his presumption and thanked him for the drink.

Chapter Eight – Scarlett

From Reading on, it was curtains up as they set about their own two-hander. Blocking out any chatter and distraction around them, they became their own leading lights, each artfully playing their part. Onlookers could observe, but woe betide them if they dared interrupt. This was their very own Brief Encounter; one she sorely hoped would come with benefits.

Chatting about all manner of topics: the novel she was reading; the box sets they were watching; their favourite restaurants in London and Devon; their shared passion for European city breaks, neither of them revealed much of their true selves. Max neglected to share anything of his family life beyond the fact that he had a nameless wife and an indeterminate number of gender undisclosed children. Scarlett bypassed sharing anything of her actuality. Neither cared. This was a double dissimulation befitting their characters.

By Taunton, Max and Scarlett had determined that she would break her journey. An overnight stay at The Southernhay would suit her just fine, and she had no hesitation when he offered to treat her to dinner and book her in. Scarlett liked the way in which Max took control of the arrangements and was hopeful that he would be just as masterful in the bedroom. She liked to mix things up a bit.

As the trolley trundled by again, he ordered two coffees, black for her and white for him. Whilst she didn't feel the need for a caffeine hit, she did acknowledge to herself that she should probably sober up a little. Two G & Ts at lunchtime was pushing it, and she was starting to feel a tad squiffy.

As the last half hour of their journey unfolded, Max busied himself pinging off messages, rescheduling arrangements, and covering his tracks. Scarlett mirrored him, making her own necessary excuses, concocting her own plausible story.

By the time the train had arrived at Exeter St David's, the duplicitous pair had firmly forged their double-dealing alliance, each seeking to exploit the other, their collusion counterbalanced.

Leaving the station, and slipping her hand into his, Scarlett felt the first thrill of flesh on flesh and, simultaneously, a sinking feeling in the pit of her stomach.

Her mind raced, pulling her between her two selves.

Suddenly stopping, she pulled herself back from the brink. Disoriented, it was as if, without warning, she was looking at her situation with completely different eyes. Confused, she struggled to make sense of where and who she actually was. Was she within or without?

"What's the matter?" he asked. "You don't look well."

She didn't feel well. She felt as if her mind and body were pulling in her different directions. Coming back to her senses, she pulled her hand out of his, "I'm sorry. I can't do this."

A dark shadow crossed Max's erstwhile equanimous face, "What do you mean, you're sorry? You were the one leading me on. I've just rearranged my whole schedule for you."

"I'm just, I'm just sorry," Scarlett's voice wavered, and her heart pounded.

Gasping to catch her breath, she steadied herself against a nearby wall, fearing her legs might give way beneath her.

"You've got to be kidding me!" he spat.

She shook her head, her hands clutching at her throat.

Chapter Eight – Scarlett

Losing patience, he jabbed at her, "Fucking prick tease."

Not so cool after all, mad Max stormed off up the steep hill without looking back.

Panic slowly subsiding, she watched as his well-tailored form retreated into the distance. Torn between desire and repulsion, fantasy and reality, her mind struggled to figure out how she had come this far.

Cast off and floundering, tears slowly trickling down her beautifully made-up face, Scarlett did an about-face and headed back to the station to continue her journey home.

Chapter Nine
Verity

Take nothing on its looks: take everything on evidence. There's no better rule.

—*Charles Dickens, Great Expectations*

The trouble with teaching nowadays is that it doesn't allow you time to learn. There's no room for growth. No space to stretch. And yet, I yearn .... I yearn to expand my horizons, push back boundaries, compose my own narrative, make all things possible.

Verity's mindset as she arrived at the station was both resigned and yet resistant, crushed and yet resurgent. Like a conflicted child pulled between two warring parents, she staggered and see-sawed as dichotomy waged war for her soul. This weekend away, coming after a few weeks of sick leave, was an opportunity for her to refashion her frame of mind and fortify herself for the return to school on Monday. Back on her feet, she must now prepare for the push forward. She had come this far. Retreat wasn't an option.

Then only a week before the Easter holidays. You can do this, Verity. Baby steps.

Collecting her scattered thoughts in an attempt to bring them into some sort of manageable order, Verity crossed the station bridge onto Platform 2. She was, she realised, actually starting to look forward to reconnecting with her old childhood friend. Whilst they hadn't seen each other since just before the start of the pandemic,

Chapter Nine – Verity

Verity was confident that, as always, their reconnection, shored up by years of shared history, both ancient and modern, would be effortless. And just what the doctor ordered.

Still feeling a little bruised, and in need of some gentle distraction on the journey to London, Verity would be careful where she sat. After her recent ordeal, she would avoid lone men, in any shape or form, and anyone who looked remotely draining. Whilst you could never really judge a book by its cover, she was confident that her radar for Lotharios, leeches and bores was suitably fine-tuned. It had certainly had its sensors tried and tested in recent months. Her husband, concerned for her well-being, had thoughtfully bought her a First Class ticket.

Oh, crap.

A fly in the ointment: Sophie from Pilates. Size six, self-absorbed, simpering Sophie.

Shit, shit, and shit.

Sophie waved enthusiastically from the opposite end of Platform 2. She was probably wondering why she hadn't seen her in class for weeks.

Sod Sophie.

Quelling a rising panic, Verity feigned myopia, double-backed over the bridge and headed for the toilets. She needed an out, and scuttling off to the toilet seemed the only option in the circumstances. Not the most salubrious of salles d'attente, Verity had been backed into an unsanitary corner. Needs must, she simply could not face exposure. It would compromise the whole journey. She'd be done for. It would be mission interruptus.

Incognito or bust.

Her train not due for another fifteen minutes, Verity reluctantly bolted herself in the grim and grimy cubicle for an uncomfortable wait, before gingerly venturing out, recrossing the bridge, and then hightailing it to First Class.

Sweaty, shaky, and somewhat relieved to have reclaimed her anonymity, Verity boarded and set about locating a suitable seat. Radar functioning well, she deftly discounted a lineup of unsuitable candidates for her companionship, before settling for a place opposite a neatly-packaged, keyboard-tapping woman similar in age and stage to her.

Sophie is probably pretty offended but what the hell...
Truth be told, she had never really cared for her much anyway. Sophie's phoney self-deprecation, and incessant smug references to how naturally oh so tiny she was, got under Verity's not size six skin. And she couldn't be the only one in class who wished Sophie would shut the hell up.

Maybe, I'll tell her one day.
For now though, skin-and-bone Sophie had been sidelined and Verity had the field. Assuming pole position in her carefully chosen seat, she wriggled out of her jacket, gathered her hair into a ponytail, took out her compact mirror, and set about blotting her face and applying a few tweaks to her make-up. A dab of Coco Mademoiselle, her signature scent, behind each ear, and she was primed. Verity's veneer.

Breaking into her preparations, a nasal Northern accent announced, "Good morning Ladies and Gentlemen, my name is Joanne, and I am your onboard host today. We will shortly be travelling the length of the carriage with refreshments for your journey with us today. We have a wide selection of hot drinks, cold drinks, sandwiches, wraps, crisps, cakes, and confectionery. We accept card payments including Google and Apple Pay.

Chapter Nine – Verity

Our First Class customers will shortly be provided with complimentary refreshments by their onboard hosts."

After a brief pause for breath, Joanne drawled on, "My colleagues and I will shortly be making our way through the train. Please ensure all elbows, legs, pets, and luggage are removed from the aisles. This is to ensure our safety and yours as we make our way through the train."

"Pretty dangerous job pushing a trolley," Verity observed. "Oops, did I say that out loud?" she laughed.

Her opposite number laughed back, revealing a hearty laugh, deep crinkles in her nose and a cheeky gap-toothed smile. Verity warmed to the unbridled character oozing out of her.

Not so neatly packaged, after all. A little looser. A little lovelier.

Emboldened by success, Verity continued, "Should be paid danger money."

"A suing nightmare too," her counterpart offered. "Just imagine the headlines. Rogue trolley killed my dog!"

"Trolley trauma at Taunton," Verity reciprocated.

Two of a kind, they pitched to and fro with increasingly outlandish and inappropriate comments, wisecracking their way into a shared experience. By the time the customer host had arrived to take their orders, Verity was wiping tears from her eyes whilst her new-found travel buddy held her head thrown back, her laughter unbridled. Verity had a front row view of her amalgam fillings.

"Anything to drink, ladies?"

Fortunately, it was not Joanne with the nasally Northern intonations. That would have finished them off.

Regaining composure, and politely ordering their refreshments, both women got their act together. As the customer host departed, wending her way along the carriage with her trolley on a potential collision course with limbs, luggage, and lives, Verity felt a burgeoning vitality course through her veins. It had been a long time since she had connected with another woman in such an uninhibited way. A long suppressed shadow flickered.

Her counterpart introduced herself, "Oh, that was so funny. You don't realise just how much I needed a good laugh this morning," she declared. "I'm Cara, by the way."

"You and me both! I'm Verity."

Unspoken issues hung heavy, neither caring to air them just now.

Sipping coffee and exchanging their reasons for travel, Cara for business and Verity for pleasure, both women packed down their own particular plights and put their best feet forward.

Divulging only perfunctory details of their lives, the intimacy they had shared through laughter, slowly ebbed. Social graces slowly stifled spontaneity. 'Twas ever thus.

Cara bemoaned the pressures of parenthood and career, whilst Verity lamented the unenviable plight of teachers today. Familiar territory, neither breaking new ground. Emerging shoots of vitality withered.

By the time they had reached the estuary approach to Exeter, both women had exhausted all pleasantries.

I can't settle for this. I need connection, however short-lived.

Cara had returned to her finger tapping, leaving Verity nowhere to go. Let down and let go, she turned her attention to the view beyond the train window, still scenic

Chapter Nine – Verity

even on this dull March morning. As she looked across the River Exe towards Exmouth, Lympstone and then Topsham, she reflected on how near, and yet so far, these places were from her vantage point. Within eyeshot, yet out of reach. Deep waters separating them from her.

Dare I dive?

Remaining on the banks, Verity contented herself, for now, with simply viewing from a distance.

At St David's, an influx of passengers boarding, Cara and Verity were obliged to shuffle over to make room for a couple of younger men, befittingly suited and booted, and clearly bigger citybound.

Dispirited, Verity acknowledged to herself that the moment had passed.

There would be no sharing of souls, no delving beneath the surface. Intimacy would not be regained, if intimacy was what it had been. Maybe it was just her imagination, but she had recognised in Cara something of a kindred spirit: a stifled dreamer, a faded lover of life, a bone-weary thrill seeker.

She had seen potential for soul sharing with the woman across from her, so near and yet so far.

But is it just my imagination? How far do my projections go?

Creating Verity's veneer was one thing, but she was, at times, unsure whether she was now gilding the lives of others. Embellishing the truth could be difficult to contain.

Whatever the unalloyed truth, it was not Verity's to expose. Flanked as she was by twenty-first century bondservants, lost in their spreadsheets, PDFs, and emails, she was well and truly hemmed in. She closed her eyes and took a deep breath, as she attempted to retreat to the deep recesses of her mind, scrambling around for space. She needed an escape route. An exit strategy. Another out.

Finding no peace within, Verity resolved to break free at Taunton. She could, at a push, manage half an hour of containment, but that would be her limit. She would make her excuses and make her getaway.

Keeping her eyes closed, she reformulated her plans in her mind. There was nothing that couldn't be changed, couldn't be altered. She wouldn't tell her husband though. It would just worry him. He had been so smothering of late.

Why worry him? He wouldn't understand, anyway.

Shortly before Taunton, she took out her phone, making a show of reading and sending messages. Leaning over to Cara, "Change of plan. My husband needs me home. His mother is really unwell, and she's taken a turn for the worse."

The lie tripped off her tongue, but her hands shook.

"Oh, I'm sorry to hear that. What a shame for you, missing your time away. I do hope she'll be okay, though."

"She's rallied a number of times before. We'll see. She's in the late stages of dementia. It's always a gamble going away at the moment. It can't be helped. I've let my friend know," Verity spoke very quickly, her short statements cracking out like bullets carefully aimed at a target. Half-truth smoke and mirrors.

Wriggling hurriedly back into the jacket she had only wriggled out of an hour before, Verity bade Cara farewell, thanked the young man who sprang nimbly out of his seat to let her pass, and headed for the train corridor, lugging her weekender bag. She needed space to recompose

Chapter Nine – Verity

herself for the change of course. Cara watched her go, not quite buying her story, not quite convinced. A little troubled.

As the train pulled in, Verity reasoned that she was doing the right thing. If she couldn't be who she wanted to be on the train, then she would need to find another setting. And if that meant drifting off course, then so be it. It was her journey, her path, and she was free to navigate it however she saw fit.

Although, I do hope he doesn't find out.

Having only ever passed through Taunton on her regular trips from Devon to London, Verity started to feel a slight pique of interest form within. It might be enlightening to discover what lay beyond the station. Or not. Peeking behind the backcloth did not always reward the curious.

Following the signs to the city centre, Verity had a good quarter of an hour to stroll along, take in her surroundings, and seek to settle her jangled nerves.

Wending her way through the ubiquitous railway neighbourhood with its profusion of pizza parlours, curry houses, barber shops, mobile phone outlets, tanning salons, and nail bars, she was pleased to eventually reach the city proper. On first appearance, it was much like any other metropolis of the South West. She noted the architecture: beauty alongside some beasts, ancient edifices shoulder to shoulder with modern, disrepair juxtaposing restoration and regeneration. Upmarket enterprises sat cheek by jowl with cheap, trashy discount stores; a number of businesses had clearly gone to the wall, the economic downturn sweeping the country reflected in forlorn shop fronts. The dullness of the day, a bank of battleship grey cloud masking the sun, did nothing to lift the city, or her mood.

I need something to eat, something hot to drink.

Picking her way through the usual suspects vying for her café custom, Verity chanced upon an inviting little tearoom.

That will do nicely.

Stepping over the threshold, she immediately had the sensation of shaking off a clinging gloom. Tastefully painted blue-grey walls, complemented by a palette of pastel pink and powder blue furnishings, embraced her warmly. Freshly roasted coffee; sweet, woody cinnamon; smoky bacon; and the saporous smell of toast: competing wafts tantalised Verity's nose and whetted her appetite. She headed straight for the sumptuous velvet wingback chair by the log burner.

Now, this really is what the doctor ordered.

The tearoom was buzzy, but not overly busy. Clutches of consumers were dotted around the space; some were clearly habitués.

Cheerful chatter and clatter.

Wriggling once more out of her jacket, Verity was starting to feel more comfortable in her own skin. She could finally breathe out. Relieved and reinvigorated, she was in a much better place than she had been so far today; more composed than when foiled on the train, and much more relaxed than when sequestered in the station toilet. In fact, this was the first opportunity she had had to fully breathe, unsmothered and unexposed, for weeks now.

It was at this point in time, before even placing her order, that Verity made the decision to postpone her visit to London, and to book herself into a hotel for the night.

Chapter Nine – Verity

It wasn't as if her actual presence in London was of any real significance.

Who would actually miss me? Who really remembers me?

Verity decided not to dwell on those thoughts. Doing so would lead her down a path she would sooner not walk. She also decided not to apprise her husband of this change in her plans. What he didn't know, wouldn't hurt him. And what she didn't reveal, couldn't hurt her. Besides, it wasn't as if she had any plans to stray or to play. She simply needed space to draw breath.

A young waitress, heavily inked and prinked, approached her table, "Hi, what can I get you? Are you having lunch or just a drink?" she asked, lisping slightly, and jiggling about her tongue stud, as she awaited Verity's response.

Having already checked out plates on a nearby table, Verity had made up her mind to broaden her horizons somewhat.

"Well, the all-day breakfast looks and smells good. I'll have it with the eggs fried, please. No sausages though, can I have extra bacon instead? It smells divine. And plenty of white toast too with butter."

Not her usual fare. She wondered what size six Sophie would say if she could see her now.

"Sure, and to drink?"

"Americano, please. Oh, and ketchup with breakfast."

No response forthcoming, the young waitress moseyed off with the order, as if she had better things to do. She probably did. Verity gazed after her, well acquainted with that sense of detachment herself.

Waiting for her order, Verity decided to check out the local hotels online. She wasn't sure quite what to expect in Taunton, but anything with a bit of character and charm within walking distance of the town centre would fit the bill for just one night. As long as it wasn't one of those budget blots on the landscape.

Verity might indulge in an all-day breakfast now and again, but she was simply too posh to Premier, and too top drawer to Travelodge. Even when crossing lines, she still had some boundaries.

With a fairly limited range of options, and plenty of availability on a dull Friday in March, she had selected and paid for a room for the night before her all-day breakfast had even made its way to her table. Secure in the knowledge that she had scant little chance of running into anyone from her regular social circles, Verity was satisfied that she had recast herself on a new, if somewhat impromptu, stage. Well-rehearsed by now, she could wing it.

Another, older woman, brought Verity's order to the table. A shapelier, and less decorated version of the younger one, she was clearly both the proprietor and Inky's mother. Both women had the same clear blue eyes, button noses, and full sensuous lips. It made sense now. Inky was reluctantly schlepping along in her mother's footsteps, searching for a way out. Self-expression solely skin deep, she would languish if she didn't break loose from the family business.

How I would have loved a daughter.

Inky's mother was far warmer than her daughter, chattering away as she served her, and ensuring everything was to her liking. Unlike Inky, she had found her niche.

"Just perfect, thanks."

Chapter Nine – Verity

"Well, enjoy," she urged, as she politely retreated, giving Verity her space.

Voraciously, Verity tucked into the plateful with such vigour that she drew glances from the women on the table opposite. Her refined outward appearance was conspicuously out of kilter with her dog-hungry devouring of the meal set before her. Suddenly aware she was drawing glances, her hackles raised.

What the hell are those two looking at?

Cornered, she caught the eye of one of the women and pointedly glared back. Verity had learned the hard way that the best form of defence is, if not exactly to attack, then to brazen it out. The other woman quickly dropped her gaze, leaving Verity to return, albeit a little more quietly, to her food. A sense of power pulsated through Verity's veins.

Bitches.

She wasn't quite sure if she had thought or hissed that; her mind had been playing tricks on her of late.

Soon after, the women shrugged on their coats, settled their bills, and left. Neither looked back at Verity.

Oops, hissed it then.

No longer the object of unwelcome scrutiny, Verity finished her all-day breakfast and enjoyed her coffee in peace. She prided herself in knowing her coffee, and this coffee was seriously good: round bodied, mellow in taste, a nutty finish and, oh yes, that crucial layer of crema. It was so good, in fact, that she ordered another with a cinnamon bun to celebrate.

Her waistband straining, she undid the button of her jeans, releasing pinched flesh.

Screw it. Who cares?

Her choice of food was more about rebellion than satisfaction. Less comfort food, more frankly my dear, I don't give a damn food.

Less hungry now, Verity picked at the bun, sipped her coffee, and turned her attention to what was going on around her. The precipitous retreat of the women on the table opposite had opened up a whole new and rather interesting tableau. A well-practised eavesdropper, Verity tuned out the clatter and chatter and tuned in to the animated conversation just a few feet away.

"Well dear, you need to break free of the addiction. It's clearly not doing you any good, is it? In my day, we didn't have this sort of issue. Things were so much simpler."

Verity recognised this type of woman straightaway. Long grey hair, no make-up, ruddy cheeks, dangly rainbow-bright earrings, vegan leather pasty shoes, and dressed head-to-toe in natural fibres, she was exactly the type of ideologue Verity would veer away from in the South Hams. Wholesome. Wholehearted. Whollier-than-thou.

The young woman sitting with her couldn't have been cut from a more dissimilar cloth. A Primani Princess, her clothes a fashion statement rather than a statement of belief, her lean frame was flattered by a figure-hugging, up-to-the-minute ensemble. Her hair, ironically in no need of adornment, was balayage blond and her undoubtedly porcelain, plump young skin had been overlaid with a touch too heavy foundation, dramatic feline flicks, and pearly lip gloss. Verity thought she looked cute.

I really would have loved a daughter.

Chapter Nine – Verity

The older woman continued to expound at length on the merits of her day.

"We weren't contactable 24/7 you know, and we didn't share every little bit of our lives with the whole wide world. And we were so much happier for it. We didn't have all these issues you young people have today."

The younger woman broke in, "Yeah, I know, but it would be really hard without having my phone on all day. You need one for everything. My whole life is on my phone. All my contacts, college stuff, everything."

"Rubbish," the abrupt retort, "I only have an old Nokia, and I manage."

"Really?" The Primani Princess's wide-eyed response.

"Yes, I mean why would I want to engage with emails and messages all day long? If I want conversation or communication, then I just go out and see someone, or just ring someone and talk to them. And, if I don't want to engage, then I just won't answer my phone. I haven't even bothered to learn to text. I still write letters from time to time. A lost art, that."

Grudgingly, Verity conceded that the older woman did have some good points. Being contactable 24/7 did have its downsides. And letter writing was a lost art form.

Still sanctimonious though.

"Yeah, you're right, I suppose," the younger woman replied, "It's just I'd miss out on so much if I didn't check my phone. All my mates are online all the time."

"I am right. And what's more, you're just frying your brain. You don't really understand what that device is doing to you. It zaps your mental and physical energy. It will deplete you. You're already welded to it."

Don't pull your punches, Grandma.

"Pardon me? Are you talking to me?" The older woman swivelled round and addressed Verity directly.

Oh shit. I said that out loud.

Primani Princess stifled a snigger.

Emboldened, Verity pushed herself up out of her ringside seat and entered the ring itself. Plumping herself down next to the Primani Princess, she looked her challenger square in the eyes.

"Well," Verity ventured, "it's just that you seem to have a whole lot of opinions. And you seem to want to share them, whether they're welcome or not."

"I'm not really sure that's any of your business. This is a private conversation, and no-one invited you to join in."

"Do you even know this girl?"

"Well, I do actually."

"Moulding her, are you then? Brainwashing her? Grooming her? " Verity was on a roll.

Primani Princess shifted awkwardly in her seat. Grasping her arm, Verity turned to her and asked, "Do you want her opinions? Is she bothering you?"

"Get off me."

The older woman stood, took a step back, and with a firm loud voice stated, "This is not appropriate. Please leave us alone now."

Verity shook her head. "No. You're full of shit and you're bullying this young woman. I won't have it," she spat.

"She's not bullying me. Please let go of my arm. You're hurting me."

Looking down at her hand, Verity realised it was now firmly clamped around the young girl's forearm. Aghast, she let go.

Chapter Nine – Verity

Head spinning, heart lurching, she took in the scene around her: the older woman standing, the young woman backing away from her, customers staring, the café owner on the phone. She thought she heard an address being relayed.

"I'm so sorry," she blurted out, "I don't know what came over me."

Hastily, she gathered her things and approached the counter to settle her bill.

"It's fine, just leave," the café owner was juggling the phone call with her instruction. As Verity backed away, she heard her say, "I've just asked her to leave."

All chatter, all clatter subdued, Verity vacated the space, tears streaming down her face. She had gone too far this time. Retreat was now her only option.

Chapter Ten
Lover

There's none so blind as they that won't see.

—Jonathan Swift

Making her way to the station to meet Tilly, Bel despaired. How could her super bright, super lovely friend be so super dim? And it wasn't the first time. Whilst Tilly might prefer to go by Matilda now, to Bel she would always be Tilly.

Silly Tilly, Bel thought wryly.

Resigned to picking up the pieces again, Bel reflected on the serendipity of her rest days falling at exactly the right time. Tilly needed her and, in spite of her frustration, Bel did like to be needed.

Her long, lean legs nimbly sidestepping passengers scurrying this way and that, watchful hoverers awaiting arrivals, stretched station staff dashing from pillar to post, and dallying time-killers trailing luggage, Bel made her way across the station. Just as she was beginning to fear Tilly hadn't shown up, she spotted her languishing beneath the statue on Platform 1. She was waiting, as arranged, under The Letter to an Unknown Soldier war memorial. She looked very small. Diminished.

In the circumstances, this sombre backdrop was a far more befitting choice than their usual Paddington Bear rendezvous. This was not a jaunty trip back to the shire for a catch up with their folks and friends. This was crisis management.

Chapter Ten – Lover

Bel and Tilly had been here before, and not that long ago.

Tilly clearly hadn't slept, her trademark sleek strawberry blonde hair looked more straw than strawberry and her blue velvet eyes, which had retreated into dark hollows, were entrenched in her pallid, bare face. On seeing Bel, Tilly remained rooted to the spot, waiting for her friend's advance. This was a far cry from their customary running embrace, shrieking laughter, and group hug with Paddington Bear. Bel girded herself for the journey ahead.

Taking Tilly in her arms, Bel hugged her close, stroked her hair, and whispered gently in her ear, "It's okay, Tils. It'll be okay."

Crumpling and sobbing, Tilly's limp and lifeless form leant into Bel, who struggled to keep her on her feet. It was as if the very essence of her friend had somehow been spirited away, leaving no more than a brittle, crumbling shell.

Bel would never understand how anyone could allow another person to get so close that they could take so much of you with them if they chose to leave. Such vulnerability was a propensity Bel had never had, and having seen so much hurt, havoc and trauma, it was one she would never consciously adopt.

"Have you eaten?" Bel asked, gently releasing Tilly from her hold and steadying her.

A shake of the head.

"Right, we've got just about enough time before we board. Let's go and grab something hot to drink and sweet to eat. It'll do you good." Ever the pragmatist.

And Bel wasn't going to take no for an answer; she steered Tilly over to a nearby kiosk so that they could grab lattes and pastries before they made their way to board the Plymouth bound train. Having only just booked their tickets, Bel reflected that it was a good job that it was midweek and mid-morning: to her relief, they were able to find seats together in the unreserved carriage. She had steered clear of the table seats. This was not the time for company or distraction. Bel needed to be tucked away with Tilly, giving her her undivided attention.

Guiding Tilly into the window seat, Bel stowed their bags and jackets in the overhead luggage rack before settling into her own seat, sugaring both lattes, and unpacking their Danish pastries.

"Tils, eat something."

With Tilly sipping and picking, and Bel swigging and devouring, the train slithered its way out of the London terminus. Weary from the middle of the night crisis call from her friend, Bel was still struggling to process what she had heard. Close friends since primary school, they may have gone their separate ways with university and career paths, but they had always been there for one another and had made a point of regular contact.

How could I have been so blind?

The revelation that Tilly had been in a new relationship was not a shock. Bel had suspected she was seeing someone since meeting up with her back in Devon at Christmas, just prior to Tilly's new year relocation to London. Concerned that her friend was on the rebound so soon after the harrowing and acrimonious split with her long-term boyfriend Shitface Simon, Bel had asked her outright if she was in a new relationship. She had even wondered, but not asked, if she had taken Shitface back. She hadn't quite believed Tilly's flat-out denial and

Chapter Ten – Lover

insistence that she would definitely be taking her time before dipping her toes back in any water again, no matter how inviting it might look.

Both now living in the outer boroughs of London, they had met up a handful of times since Christmas for some high-spirited nights out and some lazy nights in. Bel's suspicions had only persisted and grown. There was something about Tilly's furtive behaviour and the vehemence of her denials that didn't ring true with Bel. She was, after all, trained not to take things at face value.

But it was the who that was the shock. How had she failed to spot the signs? The irony of her profession was not missed on her.

"I feel if I could just talk it through with him, he'd see sense," Tilly broke into Bel's rattled ruminations.

"What the hell, Tils? That's not why we're going back. We agreed, didn't we? We'll talk with your mum and dad. They really need to know what's been going on. It affects them too. This isn't okay. It isn't okay for you, or them, quite frankly."

Bel wasn't one to mince her words. She had rounded on Tilly in her seat. Fragile or not, she wasn't about to let her friend move the goalposts.

"I know, I know, I'm just all over the place. I thought this was it. I know he loves me. If it wasn't for her, we'd be together. He pretty much said as much."

What the actual? Give me strength.

"Tils, you're not thinking straight. You haven't slept, and you've barely touched your coffee and Danish. You need to eat; you need to sleep. You need to get home and share it all with your parents. And then, we can take it from there."

Deferentially, Tilly broke off a corner of the pastry, dipped it in her latte and placed it in her mouth. Rolling it around in her mouth, she let out a sigh and laid her head on Bel's shoulder. Bel wasn't fooled. She may appear to have won this small battle, but she knew Tilly of old. She could play dead, only to ambush you later. Bel would remain vigilant, on guard.

Allowing her friend to feign snoozing on her shoulder, Bel returned to her jumbled thoughts in an attempt to fathom what on earth Tilly had been thinking. It was, she reflected, true that her friend had a track record of choosing bad boys. Even at school she'd always picked the enfants terribles. Bel had never really been able to get to the root of why. Tilly had great parents and had had a happy home life. Chris and Sarah were supportive, loving, and warm. Pretty, privileged and highly intelligent, Tilly had had a protracted head start in life. And yet, when it came to romance, she self-sabotaged. Bel suspected that deep down she liked a bit of drama.

Well, she's certainly got her drama now. A drama of epic proportions. The shit is going to well and truly hit the fan.

Bel would stick to her guns and insist that she opened up to her parents. And if Tilly refused, then Bel would tell her she would fill them in. This wasn't just about Tilly now. It was about friendships, parents, a whole village even.

Bel could and would be blunt. She knew that. Her natural no-nonsense attitude to work and life had been sharpened by her mercurial upbringing and hardened by response policing in the Met. There was nothing Bel hadn't seen, nothing she wouldn't believe, and nothing she wouldn't put past anyone. In this life, you had to be

Chapter Ten - Lover

one step ahead of the game if you wanted to survive. And ten steps if you wanted to thrive. Bel was under no illusions. Life could be a shitstorm. And you had to call out the crap. That was her job now, calling out the crap for Tilly. Blunt Bitch Bel, as she was fondly dubbed at work, was on the case.

As the train pressed forward, Bel resigned herself to the fact that her well-earned rest days were not going to be restful.

At Reading, there was a minor exodus of one-stop train hoppers and a trickling inpouring of Westcountry bound travellers. Becoming fidgety, Tilly lifted her head off Bel's shoulder, shuffled around in her seat, and abandoned all pretence of rest.

"You're right, Bel. I'll talk with mum and dad when I'm home. It's just so hard to explain to them. And embarrassing. But they'll know what to do. They always do. I've called in sick, and so I can just stay with them for the rest of the week and weekend."

Mmmm, not entirely convinced.

"It's for the best, Tils. He took advantage really. You need to tell them. He's their friend."

Bridling, Tilly was quick to retort, "He didn't take advantage. I'm twenty-eight for goodness' sake. I knew what I was doing. I knew he was married, and I knew he was older."

Yeah, pushing sixty and your dad's best mate.

"If it wasn't for her mental fragility, he would have left his wife years ago," Tilly continued. "He's only staying with her because he's worried about what she might do without him. Honestly, Bels, she even went AWOL last week and came home in a right state. Apparently, she was paranoid that the police were after her for some reason. She just wasn't making sense at all. It really scared him."

There's always a reason not to leave.

"It was never going to end well, Tilly. I just can't understand why you didn't tell me sooner."

"Because I knew you wouldn't approve. I knew you wouldn't really understand. Life is always so black and white, right and wrong for you, Bels. And I'm not you. I can't live up to your standards."

"That is just ridiculous Tils. I know I speak my mind, but I am still able to listen. I will always be there to support you, you know that. You'd do the same for me."

Even if I think you're being an absolute mug.

"I know, I know. I suppose I just feel ashamed, falling for the wrong guy again."

"You can say that again, you bloody idiot," Bel shoved Tilly playfully, and laughed a little too loudly.

Tilly laughed briefly before dissolving into a paroxysm of sobbing. Taking her hand, Bel stroked Tilly's palm, waiting for the sobs to subside. The middle-aged man in the seat across from them glanced over before averting his gaze. Bel shoved tissues into Tilly's free hand.

Eventually, heaving shoulders relaxing, gulping breaths abating, and tears ebbing, Tilly wiped her eyes and loudly blew her streaming, snotty nose. Laying her head back on Bel's shoulder, she returned to her own thoughts.

I can make him see sense. I know it's not easy for him. I can wait. He doesn't have to leave right now.

Matilda, as she now preferred to be called, and as he preferred to call her, would never have believed she was the type to fall for a married man. And yet, there had always been something about Reuben. She recalled that

Chapter Ten – Lover

even as a teenager, when she would babysit for his twin sons, she had had a bit of a thing for him. He might have been older, but he was peng. And he had always treated her like an adult, never talking down to her, never underestimating her. His boys were super cute too; Will was pretty full on and kept her on her toes, but he was very funny; Luke was softer and sweeter, and clearly had a little crush on her. She'd always liked his wife back then too. Envied her a little perhaps but liked her well enough. That was before she realised how mental she could be. Poor Reuben. No wonder he had looked for love elsewhere.

I just can't bear to think of him having to stay with her.

If Reuben hadn't confided in her, Matilda would never have known that Penelope had had mental health issues. She had always appeared so perfectly packaged, so well-polished. Whilst she had felt a little bad that she was sleeping with Penelope's husband, she had consoled herself with the knowledge that the marriage was over long before she had reappeared on their scene.

And truth be told, Penelope had always been just that little bit irritating, hadn't she? Penelope, never Penny. Never a hair out of place, Penelope. So picture perfect. So self-contained. So wrapped up in herself, actually.

And Matilda had never quite understood why Penelope had never really worked and used the brain she so clearly had. Reuben had said that Penelope lacked stickability, that she was a dreamer not a doer.

How had he stood it all these years? She's such a snowflake. He must be desperate to break free really. He just needs more of a push.

Snuggled into Bel, Matilda started to form a firmer plan in her mind. Yes, she could just wait it out. The writing was clearly on the wall for his marriage, and it would only be a matter of time before the marriage fell apart, leaving her to pick up the pieces with Reuben. And yet, she'd waited around for Simon and look where that had got her. She had matured since then; she now knew what it was like to be with a man, rather than a mere boy. And she knew she wanted this man back.

Move over, Penelope. He's mine for the taking.

Like a Kintsugi Master, Reuben had been there to pick her up and put her back together better than ever following the fiasco with Simon. He had encouraged her to learn from her mistakes, embrace her flaws and remodel her life. And what she had learnt from him and felt with him was now the pure gold seam holding her together, adding beauty to her life. She would do the same for him. She would be there for him: to revive him, restore him, reclaim him. But she would need to play her part in smashing his splintered marriage to smithereens first.

Fortified by the belief that she had more to offer than Penelope on an intellectual level, and from what Reuben had told her, on a sexual level, she would go into battle for him. And whilst she may not be quite as striking as Penelope, she had youth on her side and the assurance that Reuben hadn't really wanted to break up with her. He had been at pains to make this clear to her as he finished their relationship over affogatos in Terra Rossa.

Trust Reuben to dump me in style. Not like Simon dumping me by text, I'll give him that. At least he had the balls to tell me to my face.

If he could be brave, then so could she. Bel was right, she would have to tell her parents. But that didn't mean game over. Her parents wouldn't like it, but they would

Chapter Ten – Lover

come around eventually. She was an adult, her own person, and only she could know what was best for her right now. And that was getting Reuben back.

Bel nudged her, "Want a drink, Tils? Trolley's coming."

"Sure, tea would be good. Thanks, Bels."

Bel ordered tea for them both from the slack-jawed, standoffish steward, who looked at her like he'd been asked to whip up a Michelin star worthy soufflé.

Rude.

"Thank you, most kind sir," she gushed as he unceremoniously dumped the tea paraphernalia on her tray table. "So very kind," she continued, tapping her contactless card on the device he limply proffered, before ostentatiously flicking her long dark hair back from her face and fluttering her long lashes.

Never one to shrink into the background, Bel did like to provoke a response. Slackjaw simply grunted and torpidly moved on.

Tilly sniggered. Bel could always make her laugh.

Checking her phone, Tilly discovered a number of missed calls from Sarah. She shot off a quick message. *I'm ok mum. I'm with Bels and we're on the train. Will explain when I'm home. Please don't worry. Will check ETA and let you know. Love you x*

It was pointless asking her mum not to worry. Sarah seemed to have worrying high up on her maternal job description. Her dad was more phlegmatic, maybe she'd speak to him about the affair first. Then again, he was one of Reuben's best friends. She may as well bite the bullet and tell them together. Get it over and done with.

"Mum's worrying as usual," Tilly informed Bel.

133

Bel squeezed the teabag out of Tilly's cup, added milk and placed it on her tray table.

"Won't be long now, Tils and you'll be home."

Well, she'll have plenty to worry about now. Poor Sarah. She's only just started to recover from the fallout from that twat, Simon.

Bel was concerned that, although Tilly would be better off back home with her parents right now, the village itself could no longer be her safe haven.

What the hell was she thinking shitting on her own doorstep?

"You'll need to stay away from Reuben and Penelope though, Tils. If it comes out, there'll be an absolute shitstorm."

"I know. I will."

I won't.

"Give it some time, and you can put it behind you. You moved on from Simon, and you can move on from Reuben, Tils. You're worth so much more than them. You really need to believe that."

"I know, I know."

Tears started to form again in the corners of Tilly's red rimmed eyes. She brushed them away with the back of her hand, their saltiness stinging.

I love him, though.

"And you've got so much going for you. Your PhD's all done and dusted. You've waltzed into that research position. You rock, girl. Don't let a man fuck it all up."

Bel's hard-headed, logical approach was starting to irritate Tilly now. Whilst she would naturally reach out to her oldest confidante in a time of crisis, Bel's matter-of-fact, minimise-the-damage, move-on attitude was never really what she wanted from her. When would Bel

Chapter Ten – Lover

finally realise she only really needed her shoulder to cry on, not her great big pair of capable hands?

"You're right, Bels. I won't."

You don't understand. You never have, Bels.

There was something in the tone of Tilly's voice which made Bel seriously doubt her resolve.

I can't even.... She's soft in the head.

"Tils, promise me. Promise me, you won't do anything stupid."

Tilly's gaze drifted, her eyes finding their own drishti, drawing her energy inward, focusing on her inner purpose.

"Tils?"

"No. Yes. I promise."

As the train drew them deeper and deeper into the landscape of their childhood, they fell silent. Wrung out and talked out, each sank deeper into their own line of thought; Matilda dreaming and scheming; Bel despairing.

You can't argue with stupid.

Chapter Eleven
Romilly

For words, like Nature, half reveal
And half conceal the Soul within.

— Alfred Lord Tennyson, In Memoriam A.H.H.

It was one of those unseasonably hot pre-summer days when young and old alike peeled off their winter layers, and dared dream dreams of a settled summer to come; its estival rays on winter-weary skin tantalising and hoodwinking wishful thinkers.

As Romilly arrived at the station, happy-go-lucky sun worshippers were wiling away their waiting time basking in the mid-morning sunshine, a full spectrum of bare flesh on display. Lily-white shoulders breaking free; tender pink cleavages sizzling; tango-orange midriffs slinking and slobbing; bespeckled and befreckled limbs toasting; burnished brown beauties flaunting; and wrinkled, crinkled winter sun junkies getting their fix: a veritable particoloured palette populated the platform. Not all, however, were so enamoured of the unseasonably hot spell: synthetic suit wearers were sweating; second springers were fanning and blotting; outsized figures were dripping and mopping; overheating toddlers were whining; and the climate anxious were fretting.

Romilly's own love of the sun, tempered by her lifelong need to protect her natural porcelain complexion, was now also tinged with an inauspicious hue.

What havoc would this false season wreak?

She wasn't just thinking about the climate.

Sweeping her misgivings to one side for now, she set about finding her place on the platform, ready to board the 10.42 to London. She would follow her current trajectory, come what may.

Mutatis mutandis.

Having informed her husband that she was now safely at the station, she stashed her iPhone in her handbag, resolving not to check it for the next few hours. A temporary reprieve from accountability would enable her to set her sights on the days ahead.

Hope springs eternal.

An optimist by nature, Romilly would always tease out the best in any given scenario, no matter how dramatic, or even tragic it might be. That optimism would serve her well now as she travelled to visit her ailing mother. Unable to look the future squarely in the face, she preferred to peek around its corners. Her mother might be dying, but Romilly's Panglossian mindset would shelter her from the full weight of this reality. For now, at least.

Welcoming the train's approach as an opportunity for respite from the real world, she garnered herself for her recurring role.

First Class was fairly empty, and Romilly's reserved seat was the only one on her table until Exeter, where she would be joined by two other London bound passengers. She relished both the chance to enjoy the beautiful stretch of coastline on the ride up to Exeter without diversion, and the possibilities distraction might offer as she travelled on.

Soon after departure, the trolley host arrived with the familiar and uninspiring assortment of complimentary drinks and snacks. This host was a regular on the route, and she greeted him, as usual, ensuring she retained an air of detachment. Romilly wasn't superior, but she did like to choose her company.

"Just a black coffee, please."

Her husband having recently pointed out her expanding waistline, she had been making concerted efforts to harness it back in. More for her sake than his, or so she told herself. She had kindly refrained from mentioning his thinning hairline and chicken legs. Romilly took her coffee with a thin smile and an averted gaze.

Allowing her drink to cool, she took out her vanity mirror, smoothed her brows, applied a little lip tint, and checked her hair had not escaped its chignon. Satisfied with the look she was going for, she settled back in her seat and directed her attention to the view from the train window. Whatever the weather, whatever her mantle, the journey between her home station and Exeter St David's never failed to charm her. In her world of what ifs and maybes, she was forever grateful for the consistently beautiful backdrop to the journeys of her mind.

She particularly welcomed the push on from Newton Abbot, as the train wended its way through the Teign Estuary and up along the west bank of the River Exe. As fields of livestock gave way to shorebird-scattered mudflats, winding creeks yielded to imposing red cliffs looming large over the deep draw of the sea, and delightful dancing deer at Powderham heralded the

Chapter Eleven – Romilly

imminent approach to the outskirts of the city, she would sit back and count her blessings.

Among them, her sons Benedict and George. She loved them both deeply and equally, but differently. The younger, George, was easy to love, his gentleness and humility a magnet to those around him. The older, Benedict, was his polar opposite. He could be aloof, insensitive even, but he was engaging and funny. Like Romilly, Benedict had a keen sense of humour, and he loved a play on words. And like her, he was a crafter of words: she as a translator, he as a schoolboy blogger. Or blagger, as George would say. Blogging or blagging, he had a dedicated following and a small amount of income from his eco hero blog. Romilly suspected that economy rather than ecology was his main driver. Benedict would never pass up an opportunity for an income stream.

Whenever she passed the Parson and Clerk, she would remember Benedict's unbridled glee as a young boy whenever they were approaching Parson's Tunnel with the two rock stacks in view.

The first time she had taken the boys by train to London to visit her mother, they were still at primary school. Romilly had treated the whole thing as a big adventure for them, telling them stories and inventing games to keep them amused. En route from Newton Abbot to Dawlish, she had recounted the legend of the Parson and Clerk. Both boys had listened wide-eyed and spellbound to the grisly tale of the Devil turning the greedy clergyman and his hapless clerk to stone; Romilly had always known how to tell a tall tale. Eager and expectant, the boys were on the edge of their seats as the rock formations came into view and Romilly was able to point out exactly where they were. Suddenly, Benedict had shot up out of his seat, pointing and shrieking at a rock stack further out to sea.

Quick as a flash, he blurted out, "What's that one called that looks like a willy, mum? Mount Eroction?"

She couldn't help but laugh out loud, and draw a deep, secret pride from his razor sharp wit. She had gently, and half-heartedly, admonished him for his inappropriate behaviour on the train, more for the sake of appearances than because she actually cared. It hadn't stopped him loudly repeating his witticism every time they journeyed along that stretch of the railway line. Maturity, or more likely boredom, eventually put a stop to it. It was only much later that she told him it was actually known as Shag Rock.

Out of the mouths of babes.

Coming into Exeter, Romilly wondered who might join her. She felt ready to engage with the world again. Having, by necessity, spent the last few weeks lying low, she experienced a familiar rush of expectation. New connections, new experiences would often reinvigorate her, reboot her even. She could really do with that right now. She had missed the interplay of fantasy and reality.

At Exeter St David's, she watched with interest as a familiar cohort of passengers boarded her First Class carriage in suits, slacks, silk shirts, and other smart casuals: so very predictable. The two women who approached Romilly's table were of the smart casual ilk and, she wagered, around fifty. Both women were attractive but in very different ways. They were well-groomed and clearly moneyed. Romilly projected forward a decade.

As they took their places, one beside her, the other facing her friend, the redhead flashed her a perfectly-

Chapter Eleven - Romilly

aligned smile of recognition from across the table. Romilly smiled back warmly, registering the semblance of their hair colour and complexion, as if they were somehow of the same tribe. The curvaceous brunette next to her took out her phone, announcing to her friend that she'd let the girls know they were on their way.

"Great, make sure they know where exactly to meet us. We don't want to be traipsing around Paddington looking for them in this heat. Just tell them to meet us by M & S, and we can pick up a few bits then. Meg is bound to be starving. You can bet your life she won't have got round to having lunch before meeting us."

Her friend laughed, "Good point, Poppy will be the same. Why have lunch when mum can buy it?"

Daughters.

"My boys would be the same," Romilly cut in, uninvited.

Nodding in agreement, her red-headed counterpart graciously welcomed her into their sorority, "Oh, they're even worse. At least my daughter only eats half of what her brothers manage to put away."

Sons and a daughter. That's just not fair. Not fair. Not fair.

Her mind straying into familiar blind alleys, it took all the mental energy she could muster, to begin to subjugate such thoughts.

Always what he wanted. Always about him. Never what I needed.

Cutting into her chaotic cogitations, the redhead enquired, "Are you okay? You don't look too well."

Looking down at her fists, Romilly could see that they were clenched so tightly she had drawn blood from her left palm. She must have zoned out.

Desperate for a quick recovery, her mind whirring, she drew breath and confided sotto voce, "Oh period pain, sometimes it's really bad. Sorry, I didn't mean to alarm you."

Taking a tissue from her bag, she blotted the blood on her palm and steadied her resolve.

"Oh, you poor thing. I'm just beyond that. Dealing with the flushes now instead. Out of the frying pan and into the fire. Complete nightmare. Don't get old."

Joining the party a little late, her friend implored, "Lara, for goodness' sake, comfort the poor woman! Give her some hope. She needs something to look forward to!"

Lara laughed, "Sorry, not selling it am I? Not an easy ride being a woman."

Tried-and-true female bonding over menses, and lack thereof.

Romilly laughed too, relieved to have recovered her composure.

Introducing herself first, Romilly learned that Lara and her friend Fliss were meeting their university student daughters in London and treating them to a West End show and an overnight stay. By the time the at-seat trolley service had reached their table, they were ready to order their drinks and lunchtime refreshments en bloc, sisterhood firmly established.

"Well, to be honest, it's as much for us as them," Lara elaborated. "Who doesn't love a bit of Dirty Dancing? A bit of nostalgia for us, a bit of a treat for them."

"Oh, that's so lovely. I would have loved a daughter to do things like that with."

Don't go there. Stay on track.

Chapter Eleven – Romilly

"So, you have boys then? How old are they?" Lara enquired.

"Seventeen and sixteen. Benedict's doing A Levels and George is doing his GCSEs. It's all a bit tense in my house at the moment, as I'm sure you can imagine."

Tense is an understatement.

"You don't look old enough to have boys of that age. My boys are of a similar age."

"Child bride," Romilly smiled.

Not too far from the truth.

"Actually, Alistair and I married when I was twenty. He's a little older. I had Benedict a couple of years later, closely followed by George."

"Well, you're getting it all out of the way earlier than us. But freedom beckons, doesn't it Fliss?"

"Oh yes, and it's been a long time coming."

"So, you have other children too, then?"

"Just another daughter, she's seventeen."

Just? Just? You don't know how lucky you are. Bloody stupid cow. Stop it. Keep on track. Keep on track. You can do this. Romilly.... Romilly....

Fliss continued, "She'll be off to uni next year, too. If she knuckles down and gets the grades, that is. Bit of a free spirit she says. Bit of a slacker, I say."

"Oh, you're too harsh on her, Fliss. She'll pull it out of the bag. Lily always does, you'll see."

That's it Romilly. There you are, back on track. Focus.

"Mmm, she takes far too much after her dad, in my opinion. Too away with the fairies, living in cloud cuckoo land."

"Now, that is harsh," Lara laughed.

143

"Maybe. But thank the Lord, I don't need to put up with that anymore!"

Keen to re-enter the conversation and get in on the lowdown, Romilly ventured,

"So, you're divorced, I take it?"

There you are Romilly. Back in there.

"Separated. He's shacked up with a slip of a girl half his age. Good luck with that! I give it a year max," she scoffed, bitterness seeping through.

"He'll come to his senses, Fliss. But you'll have moved on. His loss," Lara consoled.

An icy chill rippled through Romilly, leaving her shivering in spite of the heat.

"Romilly, are you okay?" Lara was observing her from the opposite seat.

Hauling her mind back into focus once again, Romilly draped her fine cashmere cover-up around her shoulders, "It's just this wretched period. I'll be fine. It's about time I took some more ibuprofen, actually. Excuse me whilst I pop to the loo to freshen up a bit."

Grabbing her handbag, she made to move, and Fliss swiftly made way for her as she beat her temporary retreat. Both women made sympathetic noises and watched with some concern as she proceeded down the train carriage.

Safely ensconced in the train toilet, Romilly steadied herself, her hands spread wide on the sink, her bright green eyes boring into their mirror images.

Get a grip.

Practising the breathing techniques her therapist had taught her, she felt a measure of composure slowly return to both her body and her ever-fragmenting mind.

Focus.

Chapter Eleven - Romilly

By the time she had been to the toilet, washed her hands, reapplied some lip tint and tweaked her hair, Romilly was confident that she had returned from the brink. Returning to the table, she could see that Lara and Fliss were tucking into their crisps and sandwiches.

"Oh, that looks like a good idea. I need to eat, really," she commented, as Fliss made way for her to sidle back into her seat.

"Are you okay, now?" Fliss asked. "You were gone for quite a while. We were getting a little concerned."

You didn't look concerned, stuffing your face.

"Oh, I'm okay, thanks."

Taking a sip of her tea, she realised it was stone cold.

I must have been gone longer than I realised. Shit.

"Just needed to stretch my legs a bit and stand up outside the carriage," she lied, unwrapping her chicken fajita wrap. Studiously ignoring Lara's sceptical sideways glance at her friend, Romilly continued, "I'll be good again when the ibuprofen kicks in and I've got some food inside me. I'm starting to feel better already, actually."

"That's good, let's order some more drinks. You could probably do with another cuppa, couldn't you?"

"Or a G & T," Romilly laughed rather too loudly, not joking.

Catching the trolley host's attention, Lara ordered two more coffees for herself and Fliss, before deferring to Romilly.

"G & T, please."

"Oh, sod the coffee, Lara," Fliss piped up. "Let's have a G & T as well."

Hand hovering over coffee cups, the conflicted young man awaited direction.

145

"Hold the coffees," Lara smiled. "We're pushing the boat out."

"They're on me," Romilly chimed in, reaching over with her card. "I'm leading you astray, so let me pay for the privilege. No arguments."

Given no opportunity to resist, both women thanked her.

The trolley host looked directly at Romilly, shadows of confusion clearing before he handed her back her card. Evading his gaze, and latching on to her card, she gave him a curt nod by way of dismissal. Without missing a beat, she launched into a barrage of quick-fire questions aimed at drawing out more from her pro tem kinswomen.

"So, what do you both do? Do you work? Where do you live? Have you known each other for a long time? What are your daughters studying?"

Interrupting the flow, Fliss broke in, "Whoa, so many questions, so little time."

Throwing her hands up in the air, Romilly babbled, the pitch of her voice rising, "Oh, listen to me, I'm so sorry. I'm such a nosy parker. Honestly, just ignore me. I get carried away. Away with the fairies. That's what my mother would say. Just ignore me. I should mind my own business."

A short awkward silence ensued before Lara cleared her throat and proffered, "I'm an interior designer. I've been freelance since the children. And part-time. Best of both worlds, or worst of both depending on which way you look at it."

"Oh, I know exactly what you mean," Romilly pushed her way back into the game.

"So, what do you do then?" Fliss picked up the cue.

Chapter Eleven – Romilly

"I'm a freelance translator, part-time too since the boys."

Come on, Romilly.

"Wow, that sounds so interesting. I would love to speak another language," Lara enthused. "What languages do you work in?"

"Russian and French into English."

Go girl.

"Wow. Who are your main contracts?" Fliss pressed in, clearly intrigued.

"Oh, I'm not really at liberty to discuss my clients," Romilly responded and lowered her voice conspiratorially, "especially in the current climate."

And there you are.

Lara and Fliss exchanged looks over the table, as Romilly felt a surge of adrenalin course through her veins. It had been some time since she had felt on top of her game, but in this precise moment she was a champion.

"Well, that must be very interesting," Fliss responded. "And stressful at times, I imagine."

"It can be, yes. How about you though? Are you still working, Fliss?"

"No, I gave up when Poppy was born. We didn't really need the money, and Rafe wanted me at home. He's changed his tune now that he's left though," she sniped. "I volunteer a lot though and seem to be dragged on to every school and village club committee going, so I'm pretty busy," she continued, clearly keen to justify her existence.

"Oh, Fliss is never in," Lara concurred. "She's always out and about with her voluntary roles. And she is a real gatherer of waifs and strays too, aren't you, Fliss? Always sorting someone's mess out. Sometimes you're too good for your own good."

And as if, out of nowhere, Fliss had dealt the trump card.

Bloody do-gooder pipping me to the post. Who can trump a saint?

"That's so lovely," Romilly managed through gritted teeth.

Focus. You're still somebody.

Determined not to blow it, Romilly steered the conversation on to safer ground.

"Where did you study, Lara?"

As the train rolled on, the familiar sharing of stylised stories shuttled back and forth between the players.

Caetera desunt.

The conversation now flowing within safer waters, Romilly began to relax. Prying into the lives of others, presenting her prevailing truth, she had found her element.

By Reading, with another round of G & Ts under their belts, Lara, Fliss and Romilly had forged the kind of fleeting intimacy alcohol and travel could bring. With Paddington a mere half an hour away, the bonds of kinship were soon to be loosened and lost: a foregone conclusion Romilly counted on. As did Lara and Fliss, who clearly had their reservations about their slightly unhinged hanger-on.

"Oh, my goodness," Lara suddenly exclaimed. "We've not even asked what you're up to in London, Romilly. Are you there for work?"

Romilly faltered. The lie she had so carefully prepared hung heavy in her mouth. Unbidden tears pricked the corners of her eyes, and her hands started to

Chapter Eleven - Romilly

shake, fantasy and reality vying for dominance of her submerged mind.

"I'm visiting my mother. She's in a care home. She's really unwell. She'll be dead soon," Romilly's matter-of-fact, robotic truth was out of kilter with her body language.

And just like that, the mood had changed, and the scene reset.

Lara leant over as Fliss placed a hand over Romilly's trembling hand.

That feels good.

"Oh, I'm so sorry," Fliss soothed.

Lara lowered her voice and tempered her hitherto G & T buoyed tone, "That must be so hard for you. I know exactly what you're going through. I lost my mother last year. It was so hard. Still is."

It's not about you. It's about me. Or is it about me?

Romilly torn between the fabric of two minds, grappled around in the tatters of both. She didn't trust herself to talk. Letting her tears roll without check, she flopped back in her seat and shut her eyes tight, her body convulsing.

"Are you okay, Romilly? Do you want to talk? It's okay, you can talk, we're right here for you," Lara's concern was evident.

Shut the fuck up.

"Sorry, what?"

It took all that remained of Romilly to open her eyes, focus her gaze and rapid fire her responses out through a haze of tears, "I'll be okay, thanks. It just hits me sometimes. I'll just rest quietly now until Paddington. Just leave me to rest. Leave me alone."

Sinking back into the asylum of her mind, Romilly just caught sight of the thoroughly bewildered look Lara shot at a shrugging Fliss.

Fuck them.

At Paddington, she was woken by the train manager.

"We're here, Madam. Are you okay? Do you need any assistance at all?"

Disorientated and disconnected, she simply stared.

"Paddington, Madam. Are you okay? Can you hear me?"

Fragments filtering through, she slowly remembered herself.

"Oh, I'm fine. I'll be fine. So sorry, I must have fallen asleep."

"Well, if you're sure you're okay, Madam? Is there anyone we could call for you? Are you meeting anyone at the station?"

"No, I'll be fine really. Thank you so much. You're so kind."

Gathering her belongings and reassembling herself, she left Romilly behind to set off in search of her mother.

Chapter Twelve
Lola

How potent is the fancy! People are so impressionable, they can die of imagination.

—Geoffrey Chaucer

Arriving at the station already exhausted, it had taken all her mental energy to get into character. A seasoned actress, she had played her fair share of challenging parts, but this role was one she would never have chosen. It was, however, a commission she must take. An unwelcome rite of passage.

She reminded herself of her mantra, an incantation borne of necessity.

Keep on moving. Keep on keeping on.

Truth be told, it was all she could do to put one foot in front of the other, and yet she knew that remaining static was not an option. Staying still too long would be the death of her.

The heat wasn't helping. Caught in the scorching grip of a late May heatwave, she felt stifled and constricted. Yearning to break free from oppression both without and within, she felt her pulse rise and a trickle of sweat break free from under her left shoulder blade. She was momentarily glad of her new buzz cut, at least her hair wasn't sticking to her face.

Lord, help me, she beseeched a deity she had never recognised.

As a performer, she was used to assuming a persona. A great believer in method acting, she would embody her role as fully as she could; inhabiting her part, she would set her mind to speak, act, think and feel as her character would. Sometimes, immersed in her new context, she would lose connection with her own true self.

Today though, she would need to keep a grip on the essence of who she was; she would need to access it if she were to pull off this particular performance. Aware that she stood at the edge of a precipice, fantasy might be her safety harness as she flew but reality would be unavoidable when she landed back on solid ground.

Saturday mid-morning, Totnes station's Platform 2 was heaving with suitcase-schlepping and backpack-hauling travellers, day-tripping families, and teenagers in cool cliques and gawky gangs. Sidling her way through, she took her place at the end of the platform, seeking a little space to still herself before the late arrival of her train.

Leaning back against the red brick wall, she caught sight of a robin perched on metal railings a little way off.

Am I seeing things?

Recent history had taught her that she couldn't always trust her perceptions. She turned and advanced slowly, careful not to disturb. And there it sat, red-breasted and proud.

This little bird, a staple of winter landscapes, Christmas cards and festive decorations, had come to visit her in a heatwave. A less familiar sight in late spring and summer, when they had generally nestled down or flown further afield, she took this robin's fortuitous appearance as a herald of hope.

When robins appear, loved ones are near.

Chapter Twelve – Lola

Silently, she thanked the deity she doubted. She would take comfort where she could.

"The next train to arrive at Platform 2 will be the delayed 10.41 to London Paddington calling at ..."

Bringing her brutally back into the here and now, a robotic voice set out the stages of the journey she must take, clarified the delay to that journey thus far, and dangled the recompense she might expect. She could have claimed back a small fortune from GWR's Delay Repay scheme over the past year, if only she could have been bothered. Somehow, she had never got around to it. In the scheme of things, it hadn't seemed worth the trouble.

Carrying her two empty suitcases on to the train, she placed them in the luggage space before working her way through the carriage to find her seat. Three of the seats at her table were already occupied: a captive audience.

"Could you move your bag, please? That's my seat," the irritation in her voice betrayed her as she addressed the woman in the seat next to hers.

"Oh, of course. Sorry, I was miles away," her gracious reply, as she whisked her handbag up from the seat and onto her lap.

The couple opposite gave each other a look.

She sat down, sank back into her seat, and closed her eyes. She would spend some time revisiting the robin in her mind's eye. Its presence would calm her, centre her. Shortly before Newton Abbot, with the approach of the on-board refreshment trolley, she realised that she was in need of sustenance. The last few days had been a blur as she had drifted between denial and acceptance. Having hardly eaten and barely slept, she would need to fortify herself to stand a chance of pulling off her performance.

"Oh, good morning. I almost didn't recognise you," the familiar voice and friendly face of one of the regular trolley stewards was suddenly before her.

"Oh, my hair," her hand instinctively went to sweep it back, finding only fuzz.

"It suits you," he continued.

Bit familiar.

"Thank you, I'll take a black coffee, water and a flapjack, please."

Don't get too close. Back off.

"Certainly, Madam."

She accepted her order without meeting his gaze, inwardly willing him to hurry up as he served the rest of the table.

As he retreated, she set about opening the cellophane flapjack packet. Only then, did she notice that her hands were shaking violently.

"I'm not an addict," she blurted out.

Her fellow travellers, not knowing where to look, gazed out of the window or at their coffee cups.

"Or an alcoholic."

The woman opposite, clearly feeling compelled to make some response, replied, "Are you okay? Are you feeling unwell?"

"Oh no, I'm fine," she answered.

Here's my chance.

"I'm shaky because I'm having chemo. One of the unfortunate side effects. Didn't want you to think I'm a bit of a lush," she laughed, rather hollowly.

"That and hair loss," she continued. "Hence the new hairstyle."

Sympathetic looks all around lifted her spirit and empowered her to reveal more of her current self.

Chapter Twelve – Lola

"To be honest, I could do with a change anyway. I'm an actress and I have a new role on the horizon, all being well with my treatment. The new look will fit the bill really well."

"That's tough," the response from the seat opposite, "I hope your treatment is going well. Your hair really suits you, actually. You've been blessed with such good bone structure. If I shaved my hair off, I'm afraid I'd look like Yoda."

The man next to her laughed, "Well, that'd be fine by me. I've always had a bit of a thing for Star Wars characters. Admittedly, more Leia or Rey than Yoda."

The mood lightened; the company relaxed.

Sipping drinks and grazing on snacks, the group continued to engage and, in true British style, shifted to idle chit-chat about nothing in particular until, out of nowhere, the woman next to her revealed, "I'm a cancer survivor. I've been in remission for five years now. I know how tough it can be."

There's always one isn't there? Always a pretender. Always an understudy desperate to steal the limelight.

This is where her consummate acting skills really needed to come into their own. Lola was the ultimate showgirl.

"Oh really, how encouraging. Thank you for sharing that with me." Confident that she had kept even the slightest hint of sarcasm from her tone, she continued, "What type of cancer did you have? I'd love to hear your experience."

I can't think of anything worse right now.

This was going off-script. She'd have to ad lib. As she feigned hanging on every word from her fellow fighter, she was inwardly cursing the cruel hand of fortune.

This is not what I need right now. I need to be centre stage.

Self-involved and self-serving she might be, but if she couldn't play her part she might just self-implode. Deus ex machina unforthcoming, she supplied her own plot recovery.

"Do excuse me, nature calls," she announced loudly, launching herself from her seat and flouncing flamboyantly down the aisle. It was a shame she no longer had her lustrous hair to flick.

Peering with interest, and some regret, at her still unfamiliar hairless reflection in the train toilet's mottled mirror, she recomposed herself for her comeback. She was damned if she was going to be upstaged.

You can do this, Lola. Get your act together.

A bold sweep of Rouge Allure and a dab of her signature scent Coco Mademoiselle, she was ready to reclaim centre stage.

"Oh my word, nearly Exeter already, how times flies!" her overblown announcement downstage preceding her histrionic arrival back at the table.

As the train followed its course from the lower reaches of the Exe estuary into the city itself, Lola waxed lyrical, performing her own carefully crafted and well-rehearsed monologue. The battle for this character had been fierce, and she would not surrender her without a fight.

Her audience dumbstruck, she had reclaimed the spotlight.

Pulling into St David's, the woman next to her gathered her belongings in anticipation of release.

"Oh, leaving already. What a shame! So sorry, here I go again blathering on. I was so looking forward to

Chapter Twelve – Lola

hearing more of your survivor journey." She drew out 'so' just a little too long for comfort.

"Yes, sorry. Excuse me, I need to get by. I've an appointment in Exeter."

As she leant over to air kiss her, the survivor, taken aback, tried, in vain, to pull away.

"Mwah, mwah."

"Er, bye then. Have a good journey," the survivor's comments were primarily addressed to the captive couple she was leaving behind. Grimacing, she scuttled off to the exit without so much as a glance back.

"So, you're both in it for the long haul, I take it? Bearing with me until the bitter end, hopefully." Lola's laugh was loud as she slapped the table with her hand.

"Ow, shit, that hurt," she winced, having smacked her hand down far harder than she had intended.

Before either of the remaining captives could respond, an unexpected announcement came over the train PA, "Ladies and Gentlemen, we are sorry to inform you that all trains out of Exeter will now be subject to further delays."

A groan went around the carriage.

"The extreme heat we have been experiencing has caused a kink in the track between here and Tiverton Parkway. Network Rail engineers have been called to the scene and we will keep you posted when we have more news. On behalf of Great Western Railway, I would like to apologise for the delay to your journey today."

"What the actual hell, what the actual fricking hell?"

The couple opposite shifted awkwardly in their seats, the woman muttering something under her breath.

"What are you bitching about?"

"Right, that's it," her partner declared, "Sal, grab your bag, we're moving carriages."

Sal, a look of shock hollowing out her cheeks and widening her eyes, quickly complied.

She watched with disdain as they retreated.

Spineless twats.

Left in limbo, without an audience, and without direction, Lola had no option but to retreat for now into the mire of her mind, persona and person jockeying for position.

Breathe.

She wasn't sure how long she had been practising her breathwork, when she was jolted out of it with a further announcement, "Once again, Ladies and Gentlemen, we are sorry for the delay in the service from Exeter St David's to London Paddington today. We have just been informed that Network Rail Engineers could be some time before arriving at the scene. As yet, we are unaware of the extent of the damage and so we cannot give you an expected departure time. We will update you as soon as possible, and we ask for your patience with this unavoidable delay. Your safety is our priority. I will be travelling through the train now and answering any of your queries as I make my way through the carriages. Thank you for your understanding."

Groans, sighs, cursing, and phone calls reverberated around the carriage.

She took out her phone, wondering whether she should, after all, take up the unwelcome offer of a lift to London.

Twenty three missed calls.

She stashed the phone back in her handbag, unable to face looking at the call list.

Chapter Twelve – Lola

Persona receding, essence resurfacing, her mind started to revisit the past few weeks; the best of times and the worst of times. Her milestone birthday had been celebrated on the day of the King's coronation.

Why am I always upstaged?

And yet, despite the new monarch's lack of consideration, she had felt blessed. It had been wonderful to spend time with her beloved boys, both of whom had taken time out from their studies to celebrate with her. Even her husband had been on good form.

The Tiffany diamond eternity ring surely meant something, didn't it?

Life had been starting to look a little less daunting and she had told herself that maybe life did begin at forty, after all.

And then double disaster had struck. Her husband's lover's revelation a few days after her birthday had hit her hard. Yes, she had suspected. Yes, she had feared. But, no, she hadn't wanted clarification beyond all doubt. The shaky ground on which she had been teetering shifted and shook, threatening collapse. The death of her mother, just two weeks after her birthday, had then floored her, quite literally. The late night call from the care home, whilst not unexpected, had caused her legs to buckle beneath her and her mind to lose all grip. It was three days before she was able to leave her bed. It was another three days before she felt strong enough to leave the house. And now here she was en route to collect her mother's belongings. Two empty suitcases to salvage all that remained of her at the care home. It was a journey only she could make, a labour of her love.

Against all advice, and Reuben's desperate pleas, she had insisted on driving herself to the station. He had offered to drive her up to London himself, but he was the last person she wanted to comfort her right now. This was after all, just another role to play, albeit the hardest of all thus far. It would be her swan song.

And yet, the gods seemed to be conspiring against her: she'd been upstaged, the plot had twisted so far that she couldn't predict its finale, and her audience had voted with their feet.

As the train manager broke into her brooding ruminations with news of the "unavoidable cancellation of this service to London Paddington today", she felt the full force of failure hit her. Her foray had been a flop.

Storming the length of the carriage, she grabbed her cases, threw herself out onto the platform and made for the exit. Temples throbbing, linen sticking, heart racing and mind cracking, she needed to get off stage and work out what to do next. It was only much later when she had found a space alongside the river to sit, breathe and adjust that she realised why she had drawn so many odd looks. As she took out her vanity mirror to recompose her appearance, she was faced with the mascara black tracks of her tears and a Rouge Allure smear like a rude gash across her face. She looked more clown than actress.

Slowly and deliberately fixing her features, she recovered some presence of mind as she willed herself to fully surrender fantasy and admit reality.

She took out her phone and returned the last of the now thirty five missed calls, "Reuben, it's me. Can you get me? I'm stuck at Exeter. The train's been cancelled. I need you to take me to mum's."

Keep on moving. Keep on keeping on.

Chapter Thirteen
Sons

*Your children are not your children.
They are sons and daughters of Life's longing for itself.
They come through you but not from you.
And though they are with you yet they belong
not to you.*

—*Kahlil Gibran, On Children*

Luke grasped Ruby's hand as they pushed their way across the concourse, his grip so tight she had to shake him loose a little. He still couldn't believe she was his and, smitten as he was, he never wanted to let her go. Her soft beauty matched by her gentle spirit, he was grateful for her company as he travelled home for his grandmother's funeral. Ruby had never met Eva, but knowing how fond Luke was of her, she had offered to accompany him. Having only been seeing each other a couple of months, it would be a rude introduction to Luke's family.

Boarding their carriage with scant time to spare, Luke was glad he had taken up his father's offer of two First Class tickets back home. Whilst anxious to forge his own path in life, rather than rely on his family's wealth, now was not the time to quibble. Never having travelled First Class before, Ruby was curious to see how the bureaucrats, fat cats, aristocrats, and spoilt brats fared. She was also intrigued to meet Luke's twin brother. Having seen photos of Luke and Will together, she wondered if she would be able to tell them apart. Luke had insisted she would.

"This feels well weird," Ruby whispered to Luke as they settled into their seats. She wasn't solely thinking of First Class.

"We'll get free drinks and snacks in a bit, Rubes. It's a bit of a trek so stock up on whatever they offer. And then get some rest too."

Ruby stroked his arm, grateful for his attentiveness. She had been up half the night with him, as he shared something of the Aspen family dynamics ahead of her initiation. When she had met him such a short time ago in the university library, she would never have guessed the complexity of his family life. She had been drawn to his mellow demeanour and understated charm. Unlike some of the guys she came across, Luke didn't wear his good looks like a badge of honour.

Her head now full of Luke's revelations, Ruby had started to feel a little apprehensive about the days ahead in Devon, and she was trying very hard to suppress any regrets she had of offering her presence and support so readily. What was troubling her most was not so much the family's grief at the loss of a matriarch, or even the precariousness of the parents' relationship, but the current state of Luke's mother's mind. In the small hours of the night, Luke had shared his deepest fears with Ruby. He had disclosed how, over the past few months, he had become increasingly concerned whenever he spoke with his mum on the phone. And then, seeing her only last month for her birthday, his concern had only hardened. He had tried speaking with his Dad and Will, but both had downplayed her behaviour; his father blaming the toll his grandmother's dementia and

Chapter Thirteen – Sons

imminent demise was taking, Will refusing to countenance his mother could be anything less than the woman he needed. He hadn't spoken directly with his mother since his grandmother's death, as she had refused all calls. His father, cracking for once, had admitted his own alarm at his wife's behaviour and warned both his sons that their mother would look different, having shaved her hair off. Ruby had wondered why Luke hadn't confided in her sooner.

Luke, lost in his own thoughts, vacillated between grief and relief at his grandmother's passing, disquiet and apprehension about his mother, and an aching limerence with Ruby. His mother's son, his sensitive soul could be both the making and undoing of him.

"Any drinks or snacks for you both today?" The sing-song cadence of the trolley steward provided a welcome distraction for both Luke and Ruby.

"Coffee, Rubes?"

"Sure."

"Two coffees, please. Both white, no sugar. And a bottle of water each, please."

Conferring with Ruby, Luke then set about ordering a range of snacks to keep them going; he might as well get his father's money's worth. Ruby felt like royalty; not many struggling students could boast they travelled in such style.

As the steward, not much older than they were themselves, trundled onto the next table, she mentally berated the First Class brat pack.

Travelling down from Manchester, Will had had no qualms about accepting the First Class train ticket from his father, and the free coffee was great for washing down the ibuprofen to soothe his pulsating hangover headache.

Only partly regretting the excesses of the night before, his mind was revisiting the drunken, fumbling sex with Nina. He'd been vaguely aware of her since starting university, but she had not been one of those on his A list of conquests. The sex had been unexceptional but had provided him with a temporary distraction and a much-needed release ahead of the ordeal he must face. Will didn't really do difficult.

Now heading home, with nowhere to retreat, he had no option but to face up to reality; Granny Eva was dead, Dad was scared, Mum was off her rocker.

What the hell was she thinking, shaving her hair off?

Will had always valued his mother as the glamorous ever-present, unwavering backdrop to his life. As he grew and thrived, she was his facilitator as meal-provider, brow-mopper, taxi-driver, flak-taker, and champion.

What the fuck was happening to her now? And what the hell are my mates going to think when they see her around?

He felt greater anguish at the state of her pate than her mind.

Taking his phone out, Will shot off a WhatsApp message to Luke.

See you at the madhouse later! Not looking forward to this much! Groaning face emoji.

The message came in just as Luke was taking a generous bite of flapjack.

Typical Will.

Luke wouldn't reply just yet.

"All okay?" Ruby enquired.

"Yep, just Will. I'll message him later," he mumbled through his mouthful.

Chapter Thirteen – Sons

Inwardly, Luke had winced at 'madhouse'. His brother's reduction of their family's current crisis to a cheap wisecrack did not sit well with him. For Luke, their mother had always been, not only the anchor but also the sail for his life. As well as keeping him safe, she had helped him navigate his way through the trials and tribulations of childhood and adolescence and launched him into adulthood. She had enriched their childhood with her flair for storytelling and make-believe, transporting them out of the ordinary into the extraordinary, weaving fantasy into reality. The characters and plots she invented were so true to life and yet somehow otherworldly. Without her warmth, wit and imagination, his childhood would have been a whole lot harder and a lot less colourful. For Luke, his mother was a weaver of tales, a spinner of sagas, and a launcher of lives.

How had she gone so far off course?

"I'm looking forward to meeting Will," Ruby broke into Luke's introspection. "It will be so weird seeing another you."

"I keep telling you, we're polar opposites. He's my evil twin," his laughter counterfeit.

Luke was used to his twin brother stealing the limelight. More confident and less sensitive than Luke, Will would outshine him in any given scenario. Or so Luke thought. He dreaded introducing Will to Ruby, fearful he would charm and schmooze her in a way that was alien to him. It was amazing how many girls fell for it.

Please God, not Ruby.

Luke had done his best to warn Ruby about Will, without entirely slagging him off. Quelling a cresting wave of angst, he pulled Ruby close to him, kissing her gently on the forehead. He wished he could be inside her head, and truly know if the desperate need and desire he felt for her was reciprocated; they may only have been together for a matter of weeks, but life without her in it was unimaginable.

"Well, I'm still looking forward to meeting him. And your family. Although, it'll be sad and strange. I hope they'll like me, and I won't say the wrong thing."

"Oh Rubes, don't worry. You'll be fine. I'll be there for you."

"It's me who's meant to be there for you, you idiot," she laughed, elbowing him.

"I'm just glad you're with me. I'm not sure how I would feel without you." He hoped he didn't sound needy, "I mean, I know I'd cope, it's just having you with me means such a lot."

Stroking his cheek, Ruby whispered, "It'll be okay. You've got this, babe."

As the train pulled into Reading, a number of passengers gathered their belongings and made for the train corridors in anticipation of a hasty departure. Luke noticed with some pride, and no little foreboding, how a couple of the guys checked his girlfriend out en route. Ruby's shoulder-skimming hair the colour of caramel, conker-coloured eyes of fathomless depths, and delicate features drew many a second glance. Whilst Luke himself had been similarly drawn to her natural beauty, it was the honeyed tones of her voice and the incandescence of her gentle soul which had captivated him. At heart, a hopeless romantic, Luke had no doubt she was his one and only true soul mate, and he yearned for Ruby to feel the same.

Chapter Thirteen – Sons

Getting ready to change trains at Birmingham New Street, Will glanced at his phone. The blue tick tell-tale that Luke had seen his message and not replied, annoyed him.

What's his problem? We really need to stick together right now.

Will didn't understand how he and his brother could look at life so differently. Surely it must be wearing to be Luke; if only he'd loosen up a little, live a little. He was so intense, and yet so aloof with him. He wasn't the brother Will would have chosen, but he was all he had right now. In the mess that was his parents' marriage, the loss of Granny Eva, and his mother's moment of madness, they should really be there for one another.

Fuck it. I'll message again.

Aware the train was drawing into New Street, he pinged off another message before stashing his phone in his backpack.

Fucking respond, Luke. Stop being a dick. See ya later.

Grudgingly, Will acknowledged he actually needed Luke right now.

Having gone their separate ways well before leaving home for university, the twins only reassembled for family fiestas, birthday bashes, Aspen clan holidays and now, calamities. Their interaction was perfunctory, and their bond had become increasingly tenuous; Will felt a sharp twinge of regret like a knife to the gut. He would phone Luke whilst waiting at New Street for the delayed connection to Totnes.

Reading Will's second message, Luke wondered whether Will's customary sang-froid vis-à-vis any emotionally demanding situation had been unexpectedly raised to tepid. Putting his earlier irritation aside, and feeling he had been petty, he messaged back immediately.

Sorry, Will. Bad signal on train. Hope you're ok? See you later.

Five minutes later, Luke was answering Will's call and Ruby was listening closely as the brothers conducted a stop-start, time-lagging phone call. Each was speaking over the other as they attempted to ascertain how the other was, and to exchange veiled, hushed intelligence with regard to the state of play back home. Throughout the call, Luke chewed at his already sore lip, and Will eyed up a particularly hot chick a couple of feet from where he was standing.

Having established some form of expedient rapport, the brothers finished their call, Luke to nestle into Ruby and fill her in on the snippets of conversation she had not managed to overhear, and Will to sidle along the platform and strut his stuff.

Penelope's dove and Penelope's peacock.

Chapter Fourteen
Penelope

This above all: to thine own self be true,
And it must follow, as the night the day,
Thou canst not then be false to any man.

—*William Shakespeare, Hamlet*

Battered and bruised, she hunkered down, teetering on the brink of two worlds; the perfect storm having pitched her every which way, she had cut and run. Lacking both the mental energy and physical strength to venture too far afield, she was holed up just a few miles from home; the beautifully appointed hotel room looking out over a picturesque harbour, a much-needed port in a storm.

Penelope had needed a place to just be. Or not to be. This was her question.

On checking in, she had declined to make a dinner reservation, and had made it clear she was not to be disturbed under any circumstances. Peeling off her clothes, she had enveloped herself in the spa hotel's bromidic bathrobe, flopped down onto the bed and slept deeply, dead to the world beyond.

Now slowly resurfacing, the dimpsy light of dusk draping the harbour, her eyes swam, and her mind bobbed as she fought her way out of the fog of her fleeting oblivion. Her whole body bone-weary, creaked and cracked as she made her way from the bed to her overnight bag in the corner of the room. Retrieving the bottle of wine she had brought with her from Reuben's prized collection, she toyed with the idea that he might well miss his Château Lafite more than he would her.

A few weeks on from her mother's death and funeral, Penelope had barely spoken with Reuben. Even when he had driven her up to London to collect her mother's belongings, she had remained mainly mute, unable and unwilling to articulate the depth of her emotions or convey the scale of the betrayal she felt. Reuben had tried to engage with her many times but, unable to tolerate even the sound of his voice, she had pushed him away in every sense. They had been living lives more separate than ever, if living is what you could call it. Drowning in grief, regret and resentment, Penelope had been retreating ever further from Reuben and from real life.

On this particular balmy June morning, waking drenched in night terror sweat and filled with nebulous dread, she had struggled to breath. Foundering, it took every last tattered fibre of her being to haul herself out of bed, take a somewhat hit-or-miss shower and throw on the clothes she had discarded the night before. She had then set about packing the bare essentials, including a stash of unopened packs of her prescription meds, packets of paracetamol, a premium red from Reuben's wine collection, and a corkscrew, before ordering a taxi and beating her retreat.

This getaway was a far cry from the flights of fancy she had taken over the course of the last nine months. Those days were done. She was done. With nowhere left to go, she was resorting to Plan B. Deep down, she had always known this moment would come and, in spite of the ravages born of her ruptured mind, she was primed for

Chapter Fourteen - Penelope

action. This would be her moment of reckoning; a time for truth.

Truth or dare.

Uncorking the wine, Penelope poured a generous amount into a tumbler before drinking it down in one go. How Reuben would have gawped and griped. She let out a hollow laugh, imagining the look of horror on his face. She didn't have to use much imagination to conjure up that particular image; she had seen it a number of times in recent weeks.

The first rewarding rush of alcohol inducing its welcome dopamine high, Penelope's tightly drawn mind began to unfurl, ranging over recent revelations and events.

Whilst her mother had still clung to her shadow life, and Penelope had still cleaved to the lies she told herself to dodge the betrayal on her doorstep, life had been just about bearable. Her own personal odyssey, set in motion as she coveted another's more intrepid, colourful life had helped by diverting her, and sidetracking her from the bleak route she was destined to travel.

Aisling Rourke, the intrepid travel blogger, would never know what precarious wheels she had set in motion on that fateful day back in September.

But now, after months of putting on a face and showcasing facades, Penelope accepted it was time to finally face herself. She couldn't go on as she was. Her escapades, fleeting and fragmentary, had been leading her further and further into a fool's paradise. She was in danger of defaulting to delusion; maladaptive daydreaming dragging her deeper and deeper into irreality.

It seemed to Penelope that she was left with three choices: to drown in delusion, to throw herself overboard, or to seek help to swim to safer shores.

Sink, self-sabotage or swim.

These were her choices. Her decisions. And she would not leave this room until she had made headway.

Facing herself, of course, meant confronting her fears, and hauling them to the forefront of her fractured mind. She poured another tumbler of Château Lafite to mitigate the pain, blunt the trauma.

Her mind a meshwork of disordered thoughts and dislocated emotions, Penelope set about unravelling its two dominant skeins.

The first skein: Tilly and Reuben.

Titillating Tilly.

Lithe of body, fair of face, broad of mind.

Trashy Tilly.

The slip of a thing she had once upon a time welcomed in her home for wintertime Sunday lunches and summertime family barbecues. She'd even left Tilly minding the boys as Reuben had wined and dined her. The boys had loved her. She recalled how Reuben had always been careful to walk Tilly safely home to Chris and Sarah's at the other end of the village. Was he imagining how she would ripen and blossom way back then? And how, as her body tautened, her morals might loosen? Penelope's mind had been to some pretty dark places of late.

Tipsy Tilly.

Penelope's mind was thrown back to the spring. It was a Friday early evening, and Reuben was cracking open a bottle of red as she was rustling up a Teriyaki beef stir fry. Their recently remodelled, state-of-the-art kitchen was

Chapter Fourteen – Penelope

filled with sizzle and simmering smells of garlic, ginger, and honey and Penelope, hovering between realms, was trying her utmost to remain present in her own territory. Turning to take her glass from the kitchen island, she suddenly spotted Tilly through the kitchen bifolds. Weaving and wafting her way sprite-like around their back garden, she looked displaced, otherworldly. Penelope's stomach had lurched, and her throat had constricted as her mind grappled with what the hell was going to happen next. Following Penelope's gaze, panic flashed across Reuben's face. Ever on guard, and hardwired for double-dealing, he swung swiftly into action, throwing open the bifolds and closing them firmly behind him, clearly intent on heading Tilly off. Penelope had enough presence of mind to turn off the hob before gripping fast to the kitchen island, fearful of being swept off into waters deep and dark.

    She wasn't sure how long she had been stranded there, but when Reuben returned the Teriyaki was as cold and congealed as her spirit. Her limbs like lead and her heart like a sunken stone, Reuben had taken control of the situation and ushered her into the lounge before calmly concocting his canard: Tilly had been a bit drunk after a silly row with her parents and so she was seeking refuge with them; he had felt it best to take her home to Chris and Sarah to sleep it off; Tilly had been a little unstable of late following that break-up last year with that idiot of a boyfriend. Penelope had hungrily, gratefully even, swallowed the lie and agreed to him ordering an Indian takeaway. That night, for the very first time, truth had lodged firmly somewhere in the back of her mind; she just wasn't ready to allow it to travel forward. Reuben had ordered their meal, topped up her wine, and made love to her more tenderly than he had in a very long while.

Tell-tale Tilly.

Hard truth trampled soft lies a few days after Penelope's fortieth birthday. Her body felt its cold chill, her mind reeling back to the scene. She pulled the duvet up around her as she took another generous glug of wine and reconjured that fateful juncture.

Following the boys' brief stopover for her birthday celebrations, she was stripping the beds when the doorbell rang. Tilly had stood, sober this time, and unwavering on her doorstep, clearly drunk on her own agenda. Her first instinct was to close the door, close her mind, and refuse to let Tilly over the threshold into her home and into her inner world. Tilly clearly had other ideas as she strode straight in, announcing they really needed to talk about Reuben.

They hadn't talked. Tilly had talked as Penelope had half listened, rendered speechless, as her husband's lover mercilessly spilt all the juicy beans she had. Dying inside, Penelope willed her unwilling mind to transport her into another reality. When Tilly eventually left, Penelope had crumpled, parting words like bullets at point blank range.

"He's only still with you because you're mental. Let him go. Let him have a life, Penelope."

Was this really her Reuben who had just a few days ago made such a show of celebrating her, presenting her with the most exquisite eternity ring, and professing his undying love for her alone? Was this her Reuben in lust with a nymph, young enough to be his daughter? A daughter he had never wanted her to bear. Of course, it was. Truth had finally, irrevocably broken through, violating the forefront of her mind.

Chapter Fourteen – Penelope

Reuben had returned home from his office early, clearly tipped off and visibly panic-stricken, to find Penelope dishevelled and prostrate on the parquet in the hall. Explanations, justifications, and regret had fallen on deaf ears, Penelope was imploding fast. It had taken all his strength to move her to the sofa, where she lay stupefied as he retrieved diazepam from her bag and practically pushed it down her throat. He was now hanging by a thread, and he knew it.

Out of nowhere, Penelope felt a hunger inside. She hadn't felt physical hunger for some time now. Over the last few weeks, she had eaten sporadically and more out of necessity than desire; her naturally slim frame now more ravaged than ravishing. Locating the hotel phone, she called room service for a Club sandwich and a bottle of Malbec. Her bread, her wine. It might well be her last supper. Whatever it would be, she needed fortification before grappling with the second skein.

"We'll be with you in twenty minutes, Madam."

Rising from the bed, Penelope felt light of head but also a little lighter of spirit having veraciously unpicked the tangled triangle Reuben had constructed. She took off her robe and stepped under the shower, allowing the full force of the water to wash over her, as she shampooed and soaped herself. Balm for the body, purge for the mind. By the time room service arrived, she felt unexpectedly more composed than she had for some time.

The Club sandwich smelt and tasted divine as she devoured it inelegantly, mayo dribbling from the corner of her mouth.

Oh, the joys of eating alone. So good.

And a measure of joy it was, she felt it rising. Alone, unencumbered, and unobserved, a sliver of joy had somehow transcended her heartbreak. She wiped her mouth on the back of her bathrobe sleeve and poured the remains of the first bottle of wine into the wine glass which had been brought with her second, less prestigious bottle, and her thoughts turned to her mother.

The second skein: Eva.

Ever her torchbearer, Penelope's mother had always inspired her and stood by her, spurring her on until, eventually, she couldn't. Eva had raised her daughter well, and when Penelope had needed her, she had been present, supportive, and wise. Bringing her up alone, Eva had thrown herself into her parenting, laying down a bedrock of security, stability and consistency, whilst overlaying it with a whole lot of fun. She hadn't been perfect of course, and the vagaries of Penelope's adolescence had tried and tested Eva's patience many a time. Sparks could and would fly. And yet, as much as it could be stretched and strained, their bond had always held fast, and Penelope had never doubted her mother's devotion. Even when Penelope could sense disappointment in her choice of Reuben over Classics at Durham, Eva had nobly swallowed her disapproval and worked hard to embrace her daughter's decision.

Eva *mater familias*. Encouraging Eva.

Eva had always urged Penelope to dream big. A romantic at heart, she had fostered and affirmed her daughter's vivid imagination. The weighty woes of the world were far too great to bear if one didn't stretch the imagination and create space for the mind to wander at will. Penelope's childhood had been high-spirited and, at times, whimsical; her mother's effervescence adding zing and zest to their lives.

One of the greatest pleasures of Penelope's life was her mother's bond with her boys. She had doted on them to the point of spoiling them and they, in turn, had loved their gift-bearing, game-making, Gin-swilling, up-for-anything Granny Eva.

Eva *compos mentis*. Effervescent Eva.

It was almost nine years ago now, that Penelope had sat clasping her mother's hand in the consultant's office as he delivered the dreaded diagnosis they had both tried so very hard to discount. Undeniably shaken, Eva's first instinct had characteristically been to console her daughter. In the intervening years, Penelope had felt like a helpless, hapless bystander as her mother was propelled on through a tortuous, torturous passage. Eva's journey at first slow and, at times, halting, gradually gathered speed until she had receded into the distance, out of reach. Her ever-present, ever-loving mother had slowly faded into a misty, murky vestige of who she once was.

Eva *non compos mentis*. Evaporating Eva.

Penelope took a large swig of Malbec as she forced her mind open, prising out fears she would rather not face.

Memento mori.

Staring death in the face, Penelope knew she must meet its keen gaze head on. In order to weigh up her own mortality, she first needed to process the rigours of recent weeks. Eva's death, close on the heels of Tilly's devastating disclosure, had rendered her virtually catatonic for a few days, unable even to communicate with her beloved boys. Collecting her mother's belongings and attending the funeral Eva had, of course, meticulously pre-planned, had frazzled every last shred of Penelope's nerves. She had even left the organisation of the service and wake to Reuben, unable to countenance it herself.

Eva *mortuus.* Extinct Eva.

Alone now, Penelope allowed herself to feel, to cry, to rage, to whimper, to wail. For trust broken. For loves lost.

Pitching, lurching, thrashing, reeling; her mind, body, and soul adrift on the darkest of waters, she prayed to the deity she doubted for solace, for salvation. As a vessel, she was at the very end of herself, of her selves; Penelope, Emma, Amelia, Tori, Ella, Scarlett, Verity, Romilly, and Lola. All her what ifs, why nots, and might have beens; shifting selfhoods gradually remoulding and replacing the core of who she was. Like Theseus' ship, her identity moot.

Were she to meet her Maker now, it wouldn't be so much who the Maker would be, but who the Maker might meet.

Who the hell am I?

She wasn't sure how long she had remained in a state of frantic flux, but as her mind finally came to a place of stillness, the sunlit crown of dawn was rising over a tranquil, rippleless harbour and her decision had been made.

She would swim.

Chapter Fifteen
Weaver

But you, brave and adept from this day on . . .
there's hope that you will reach your goal. . .
the journey that stirs you now is not far off.

—Homer, The Odyssey, Book 2

It had been a long and hot, sticky summer, and Penelope was glad of the storm. Rattletrap sash windows humming, rods of heavy rain drumming, flashes of lightning coruscating darkened skies, and the cymbaling of overhead thunderclaps; Penelope marvelled at the spectacular grand finale performance for her send off. A fitting farewell.

I'm ready.

In the weeks since her self-admission to the private psychiatric unit in Bristol, Penelope had undertaken the single most arduous and enlightening journey of her adult life. Covering ground old and new, she had scaled heady heights, plunged into deep dark valleys, forged ahead through badlands and sadlands and fought her way through murky mires and stormy waters. Gamely navigating uncharted territories, her determination had never wavered, her desired destination point foreordained.

Dum spiro spero.

Grateful for the time and space she had been granted to disentangle and repair her riven mind, Penelope was acutely aware of the privilege of her position; money didn't only open doors, it could also open minds. Her mind, now open to possibilities and primed for purpose, she was well-prepared for her comeback. It wouldn't be any old comeback, and it wouldn't necessarily be the comeback hoped for by those around her. Penelope wasn't simply bouncing back, she was vaulting.

Penelope upgrading.

As Reuben drove through the leafy lanes leading to the hospital, he felt the familiar knot in his stomach constrict and dilate, his mind oscillating between angst and hope. Having taken a summer sabbatical from his business, he had had plenty of time to do some soul searching of his own. Initially lamenting his wife's mental health crisis, and bitterly blaming it for ripping the very heart out of his carefully constructed shiny nuclear family, he had slowly moved towards a place of accepting his own part in the decimation of his dream. He had not only seen the signs, he had run roughshod over them, choosing distraction and gratification over dedication. He had done his fair share of breast beating, recognising that the brutal tearing of the veil between the lives they once had and the lives they would now be destined to lead might have been avoided if he had acted sooner. And acted more responsibly.

Resolving to reform, Reuben had cut all ties with Matilda, relinquished his broken friendship with Chris and Sarah and, with Penelope's consent, put their family home on the market. They would move wherever, and he would do whatever to rebuild. And yet, he couldn't shake off the nagging dread that the hole in the fabric of their family might never be fully repaired.

Reuben ruing.

Back in the family home, Will and Luke busied themselves with preparations for their mother's

Chapter Fifteen – Weaver

homecoming. No fanfare, no legendary Aspen family fiesta, this celebration would be muted, gentle. Bound by blood, history and now trauma, both boys were working alongside one another making preparations for the evening meal. They had just finished beautifying rooms with an array of seasonal flowers their mother would love, and Reuben had ordered in. Swathes of colour and a spectrum of scents filled the house: the citrusy fresh fragrance of pastel sweet peas in the kitchen; the heady aroma of sumptuous yellow tea roses in the sitting room, a waft of vanilla-chocolate cosmos in the entrance hall, and scentless delicate white Japanese anemones in the master bedroom, Reuben's renowned attention to detail had been set to impress, to atone.

As they rinsed and scrubbed, sliced and diced, the twins chatted lightly whilst prepping the evening's tagine. Dissembling, determined to be upbeat, they danced around the enormous elephant in the room. The last few months had taken a heavy toll on Will and Luke in similar, yet different, ways. The shock and impact of Penelope's decline, diagnosis, and hospitalisation had devastated them both. In their own way, each of the boys had taken for granted the weft and warp of their mother's presence in their lives, and when they realised just how close they had come to losing her, neither had coped well. Luke's darkest fears for his mother had finally been realised, unravelling him, and leaving him at the mercy of deep despair and crippling anxiety; Will, who had assembled every barrier he could to shield himself from the ugly truth, was pitched into a chilling topsy-turvy world without stabilisers. In the immediate aftermath of their mother's implosion, each responded true to form. Luke had barely slept, barely eaten, barely spoken. Ruby, right beside him, had supported him as best she could, eventually blackmailing him with threats of her own desertion if he didn't seek help from the doctor. Ruby hadn't really signed up for disaster management, but she was doing the best she could. Will, in contrast, had scrambled down a sybaritic rabbit hole, drinking himself into stupors, and spending whole nights at it like the proverbial rabbit.

By the end of July, Reuben had taken steps to mitigate the damage sustained by his fractured family unit, uncharacteristically insisting both boys come back for the remainder of their university vacation and abandon their August plans. Luke, warily embarking on a course of fluoxetine, had wearily agreed, much to Ruby's relief. Will had railed, and then relented after a particularly prolonged hangover.

The weeks in the family home leading up to Penelope's return had been both blessing and curse as Reuben, Will and Luke regrouped, the ties binding them occasionally strengthened and often strained. Now hovering between relief and trepidation in the face of their mother's re-entry into their world, Will and Luke chose light relief over heavy heart-to-hearts.

Will sidestepping. Luke shrinking.

At the other end of the village, Sarah had just taken a call from her daughter. No-one had told her that parenthood didn't get any easier the older your offspring were. As she put the kettle on, she toyed with the idea of reinforcing her tea with a generous slug of whisky; alcohol o'clock was getting earlier and earlier these days. Resolutely resisting temptation, she consoled herself instead with half of a large bar of Dairy Milk and rang Chris. As his phone went to voicemail, she left a snarky message, simultaneously resenting and envying his

Chapter Fifteen – Weaver

capacity to detach at will from the shitstorm swirling around them. By nature, an empath and a fixer, Sarah had reached the unwelcome conclusion that her patience tank was nigh on empty and any attempt by her to mend or mitigate the situation was futile: Matilda, in full-blown denial, was waiting for Reuben to come to his senses; Reuben was a snake in the grass who had betrayed their friendship as well as his wife and family; and Penelope's friendship was forever lost to her.

Matilda deluded. Chris blocking. Sarah spent.

Penelope watched dispassionately as Reuben's Tesla advanced effortlessly through the torrential rain and up the sweeping drive to the hospital's forecourt. He had been visiting weekly as soon as he was permitted to, and she was now able to bear his presence, albeit in limited doses.

In spite of the turbulent weather conditions, the drive back home to Devon was straightforward, the roads relatively clear, and the conversation pedestrian. Careful not to disturb his wife's hard-won equilibrium, Reuben stuck to safe subjects: traffic delays on the way up; the rising cost of takeout coffee; the boys preparing dinner. Penelope reciprocated, careful not to burst her husband's bubble. She looked forward to seeing Will and Luke, both of whom she had banned from visiting her in Bristol; more for her sake than theirs. Unable to bear the thought of them visiting her in a psychiatric hospital, she had declined Reuben's petitions on their behalf. She had, of course, recognised that she was putting her own needs before those of her sons and, as much as she loved them, somewhere deep inside she rejoiced in her resolve .

Penelope was not only well on the road to recovery, she was also branching out.

Per ardua ad astra.

Having faced her long-suppressed fears and deep-rooted insecurities, Penelope had finally worked on transforming from the inside out. The journeys she had taken over the past year, both physically and of the mind, had shown her that other routes, imagined lives, were not her holy grail. Masking, feigning, fantasising, recasting: she had been no more than an imposter, a pretender, a deceiver. Finally face to face with Penelope, she had begun to accept who she actually was and had realised that just might not be who she was expected to be. Imperfect, scarred, at peace. The time had come for Penelope to set her own agenda.

During her time in hospital, she had given much thought to the name her mother had given her.

Penelope: dream weaver, faithful wife.

How prescient her mother had been. And yet, now was the time to shake off the epithets, slough off her old identity. This time, from the inside out.

Penelope shedding.

She had drawn up her exit strategy well in advance. She would enjoy her first night home with her boys and with Reuben, and she would slot back into her prescribed role and bide her time, knowing her escape route had been meticulously planned. She had already instructed her solicitor and informed him that the family home would soon be on the market. She would later inform the boys of her intentions before she broke the news of her decision to divorce him to Reuben; she had no qualms about him being the last to know.

And she was under no illusion, the grass beyond would not necessarily be greener, but it would be a different shade of green, and one which may just suit her complexion better.

Chapter Fifteen – Weaver

Penelope would always be a weaver but this time of realities. Extricating herself from the tatters of her life with Reuben, she would be free to weave her own tapestry, one in which her feckless husband was no longer the protagonist. She would be no wife of Ulysses, a treasured possession, weaving and waiting whilst he ventured far and wide.

Mindful of the ties which still bound her to her old life, her sons, her friends, and acquaintances, she appreciated that the choice was hers alone to determine how tight or loose these ties should be. And in the case of some acquaintances, whether they might be entirely severed.

Crossing the border into Devon, she felt butterflies dance in her stomach as she anticipated soon holding, caressing, kissing her boys. And yet, even as she visualised pulling them close, she was also preparing to mentally loosen the cords tying them to her. For them to fly like arrows, she needed to release them from the straining quiver in which she held them. Like her mother had with her, she needed to let them go, set them free to create new bonds, and weave their own tapestries, hopeful that she may feature in roles both old and new.

She was thankful to the deity to whom she had cried out for salvation; for healing, for clarity, and for strength to face the days to come. Whatever might lie ahead, wherever this new dawn might lead her, she would sail her own course leaving her family to embark on odysseys of their own.

Entering the village, Penelope turned to look at Reuben, squeezed his hand lightly and smiled.

Penelope weaving.

About the Author

Rebecca Southgate Williams is a debut novelist who loves to challenge our perceptions of reality and peel away the masks we wear to reveal what lies behind them. With an Honours Degree in French and German, a Master's Degree in Library and Information Studies, and a Certificate in Translation, she has a long-held appreciation of the scope and power of the written word. Whether used to obfuscate or reveal, tear down or build up, repress or transform, words can create so many different narratives and perspectives. Her love of both classical literature and modern psychological dramas led her to the idea of creating a modern-day odyssey to explore the landscapes we travel, both in body and mind. A mother of three adult children, she currently works in the charity sector and lives in Cornwall with her husband and her younger son.

Acknowledgements

So many people have encouraged me to write my first novel and cheered me on along the way. I am deeply grateful to each of them.

Thank you to my dear friend Rachel David, for being the first to listen to my idea and laugh only when appropriate.

Thank you to the wonderful women in my family who have loved, supported, listened, and read some or all of my work: my mum, Lesley Paterson, my daughter, Isabelle Sadler, and my sister, Jo Southgate. I am grateful, in particular, to my mum for her belief in my ability to write, and to my late mother-in-law, Joy Williams, who was so excited about my debut novel.

Thank you to my lovely friends for reading, offering suggestions, and cheering me on: Jo Wade, Rachel (again), Emily White, Sian Jones (my number 1 flatterer and sounding board!), Liz Worham, and Sarah Wood. Without friends like you in my life, my own personal odyssey would not have been so blessed.

I am very grateful to Paul Dixon for his time and professional expertise in producing the excellent photography for the book cover. And to my daughter, Isabelle, for her modelling skills! Thank you also to Hannah Foden Dixon for her skill and patience in designing the cover layout. I am also grateful for their support and friendship.

And last, but by no means least, thank you to my husband Neil Williams, who read through for me, offered suggestions, and spurred me on, and to my stepfather, Jack Paterson, who has always supported me and nitpicked over grammar.

Printed in Great Britain
by Amazon